MAY DAY

MAY DAY

James Beeson

This is a work of fiction. All of the characters, names, incidents, organizations, and dialogue in this novel are either the products of the author's imagination or are used fictitiously.

Any people depicted in stock imagery provided by Getty Images are models, and such images are being used for illustrative purposes only.
Certain stock imagery © Getty Images.

Print information available on the last page.

Rev. date: 11/14/2018

To order additional copies of this book, contact:
Xlibris
1-888-795-4274
www.Xlibris.com
Orders@Xlibris.com
787192

The resemblance of any character in this book to any living, deceased, or yet-to-be-born entity is strictly coincidental.

Rebecca,
Prose is like tennis without a net,
But this time that's what you get.
I love you more than life itself and
Will till my last spark is extinguished.

CHAPTER ONE

Mr. and Mrs. Stover only had one child. Both parents were typical Anglo-Saxon specimens—pale, pallid, and pasty, along with a major sunburn tendency. When their daughter was born, she was a healthy normal child. Her skin had an attractive olive color, which surprised the obstetrician and parents alike. They sought, by way of a DNA profile, an explanation of her curious cutaneous hue. There were no questions as to the paternity there, at least voiced.

Mr. and Mrs. Stover were mostly Anglo-Saxon, but there was a 25 percent Mexican contribution. That solved their academic interests. Good old recessive genes at work.

Their daughter did well in school and had a coterie of friends and acquaintances. She pointed to a career in nursing early on and was readily accepted into a local nurses training program as she was about at an end of her high school tour.

Everything was going well for her until she attended a night soccer game at her school. She was sitting beside a group of high school football players who were busy drinking their "Coke" from the contents of a brown paper bag. They offered her a sip. She did so and found it sweet and tasty. "We have another bag if we finish this one. Have some more," one boy offered. After the third swig, May knew she'd had too much. But it was too late. She felt light-headed and a little bit nauseated, so she left the stands and went beneath them in case she threw up. The four boys followed her, initially to be sure she was all right. When they were assured she was, one of the boys gave her a big kiss. She didn't resist, so the other three did likewise. This rapidly morphed into groping and on to a gang rape. When she resisted, one boy covered her mouth with his hand while another had his way with her. They took turns doing so as they sequentially assaulted her. When they were through, she was alert enough to know what had happened and who were involved. Not really knowing just what to do next, the boys led her back to the stands and left the stadium.

A teacher nearby saw her obviously impaired movements along with an increasing amount of tears. "What's the matter, May?"

"I was just raped by four of your students," she answered. After a brief moment of disbelief, the teacher did the proper thing by calling her parents on a cell phone, informing them of her status and asking them to meet her at the hospital. She assumed them May was all right except for the obvious.

With the criminal overtones involved, May was sent to the head of the line at the ER. Examination revealed no injuries other than for the traumatic hymenotomy bleeding, which had ceased. The police arrived just after the parents. May was now quite lucid and gave her account of what had transpired and who the culprits were.

Over the protestations of the boys' parents, the four boys were arrested and incarcerated. They had decided not to deny the event entirely but to contend it was all consensual. The four boys were bailed out the next morning.

DNA tests revealed a conglomerate of three of the boys. They didn't know why number 4 didn't register.

CHAPTER TWO

Naturally, the assault was the main subject for the school kids' social media. A few even talked about it. Not unexpectedly, the school's boys "knew" it had been all consensual and the girls "knew" it had not been consensual.

A week later it was old news and fading, but soon there was going to be a trial. And that would rev it all up again.

May had been in the safe segment of her menstrual cycle, so pregnancy wasn't an issue. By month's end, May was able to resume her dedicated studying and get on with her life. She did make a vow to herself that she would have her revenge when the time was right. Maybe the upcoming trial would lead to ample revenge. Maybe it wouldn't.

Helen Stover had initially prevailed upon her husband not to attempt any reprisal on the offending boys. That would only get him jail time. May admonished him likewise.

There were several meetings of the four boys together and with their parents. After a brief hell-raising with them for their collective indiscretion, they all got their wagons in a circle, being sure they were all on the same page. Conflicting versions were sure ways to adversely affect the outcome of the trial where they were being tried as adults.

Six weeks later the trial began. The prosecuting attorney contended that this was a gang rape, pure and simple—well, maybe not all that "pure." He gave impassioned opening remarks and demanded that justice be served.

The expensive defendants' attorney oozed sartorial and affable splendor. If this was not consensual, where were her injuries? It was her word against the words of the four tastefully dressed, modestly positioned sober young men—oh, and they all had fresh conservative haircuts.

The ER doctor admitted that there were no bruises on the young lady. Nobody in the stands heard calls for help. A guilty decision would effectively ruin the lives of these four promising young men. They never ever would have done such a thing without her cooperation.

The boys had been coached that one smirk could ruin their chances. They believed it. The DNA expert wasn't needed for testimony. Consensual.

May kept her head down most of the time at the trial. When she occasionally did look up, she would quietly glare at the boys. They were careful not to make any eye contact with her.

It was the lack of bruises that determined the outcome of the trial. Not guilty! May's parents were outraged. May only smiled wryly and thought again that revenge would be hers, but at a time and place of her choosing.

CHAPTER THREE

The Stovers got on with their lives. The assault became old news. May came to act as if nothing had happened—operative word being *act*. Externally, she was her old self. Internally, she was quietly forming long-range plans to repay her four attackers.

May graduated third in her class. She got hugs from her girlfriends. "Be sure to stay in touch," she was told. She had not attended the senior prom. Nobody had asked her. She didn't care.

In the small interval between her high school graduation and the commencement of her nursing studies, she got a job as a waitress at a restaurant near her home. With her general beauty, augmented by her olive-colored skin, she was well received by patrons as well as coworkers. A few of each attempted to hit on her. She courteously rejected them all.

Her nursing program was financed by a scholarship, student loans, and whatever her parents could afford. It worked.

Being innately smart and thoroughly dedicated, May led her class from beginning to end, some three years later. Her school didn't award participation trophies, so her excellence was featured. Three different hospitals tried to recruit her. She picked St. Miguel's.

She was pleasantly surprised when she heard that Don Barney was doing an externship at her hospital. Some premed students do that to be able to add that to their medical school applications. He would be there a couple of months, she heard. That should give her enough time. It took all her sequestered three-thousand dollars to purchase from a very unsavory person a pistol with a silencer on it, and no, she didn't need any drugs at the time.

It took some doing to find times when her schedule and Don's overlapped. Difficult but not impossible. Don was unaware of May's employment at the hospital. Too bad.

Chapter Four

Don Barney had kept in touch, since their graduation, with his three fellow football friends. Sam Sales was in prelaw down at Gainesville. Vic Post was in the business school mode there also. Wallace Tenor was enrolled at Jacksonville University in their fine arts program.

Their interchanges never included anything about May or the incident. They felt they were collectively upwardly mobile. Stay out of trouble, and let the past bury the past. Nowhere to go but up.

May unobtrusively monitored Don's actions. Typically, he came in at seven in the morning and departed about four. There were too many people all over the place then, including shift-change personnel. Her own schedule was usually seven to four also.

Days passed. May was barely able to tend to her patients, what with the pistol languishing in her purse. It would need to appear to have been a mugging. She couldn't do that in broad daylight. There was no opportunity. The days dwindled down to a precious few, and then he was gone. She rationalized that completion of her project was not time dependent.

Wallace Tenor would give her home-court advantage. *Wonder what old Wally's doing these days?* she wondered.

CHAPTER FIVE

May decided she needed more time to implement her crusade. She would need a back door, among other things. Another nurse at the hospital, about her age, developed encephalitis, which was quickly fatal. May knew of her but didn't really know her. May hacked the hospital's computer system and downloaded everything they had about their newly deceased employee. A back door! She would maintain her nursing license and the late nurse's license also. An anticipatory alias, if necessary. At the girl's funeral, May sat next to another nurse from their hospital whom she had seen before but didn't know. They struck up a conversation after the funeral service.

"Did you know her well?" May asked.

"No, not really. How about you?"

"No, me neither. I understand she was well-liked by the people that worked with her. Sad affair."

"Indeed. Just curious, are you Latino? Your skin is so lovely."

"Twenty percent, they say. Both of my parents are white as white can be."

"Are you a lesbian, by chance?"

"No. Not by chance or design. Are you?"

"Yeah, I am. Not the dominatrix variety. I heard you were assaulted a few years ago—that didn't sour you on men?"

"On those men, yes. I try not to generalize."

"How about we just be friends?"

"I'd like that. Real friends are always in short supply when the going gets tough. I found that out a few years ago. As to your persuasion, I don't care what consenting adults do. Dealer's choice."

"Want to have dinner with me this evening—just friends?"

"Love to. Oh, by the way, what's your name?"

"Janis Barkely. Doesn't come trippingly off the tongue, does it?"

"I'm May to one an' all—Stover. No relation to the candy people or that old cartoon character Smokey."

"Did you ever smoke, speaking of which?"

"No. Willfully taking the products of combustion into your lungs always seemed idiotic to me."

"You know, I have said the same thing. Now a measured dollop of an alcoholic beverage once in a while can be a social lubricant."

"I was lubricated, as you put it, several years ago. One glass of wine, and a small glass at that, is my limit now."

"I can usually handle two glasses, but I don't do any driving if I do."

"Do you have an up-to-date car?"

"If you're speaking in decades, yes—twelve-year-old Ford. Still dependable though. How about you?"

"Mine's twelve years old also. I want a new one with all those bells and whistles. Rearview camera, front-end collision avoidance, push-button ignition, no gas cap—"

"What do you mean by 'no gas cap'?"

"There's a metal flap there that a delivery nozzle can push up, and it reseats when you're done."

"I want a new car too!"

Chapter Six

The next free day, May visited the Ford showroom. The salesmen there fell all over one another to get to that olive-skinned beauty. The winner was a handsome twenty-five-year-old.

"How can we help you, ma'am?"

"I'm too young for a 'ma'am.' May Stover. I'm interested in a new four-door sedan. My current car is twelve years old."

"Well, we do have a bunch of those here, but we won't next year."

"Why not?"

"The Ford Company, in its infinite wisdom, is not going to make that model anymore."

"Well then, I'd better get one pretty quick."

"I was thinking the very same thing. What color were you thinking about?"

"Off-white, I guess."

"That's the biggest seller here. Let's visit the lot outside."

It was a short walk to the new cars, and a sea of them there was.

"How about this one?" The salesman pointed to one fitting her description.

"Sweet! What's it cost?"

"Don't pay any attention to the paper on the window. That's for show. Somewhere around forty."

"That would be thousand?"

The salesman smiled. "Yes, May."

"Do you finance the cars here?"

"We wouldn't sell very many if we didn't."

"The warranty is three years, isn't it?"

"That's right."

"What kind of a down payment would you need?"

"Could you handle 10 percent?"

"Maybe. I'm a gainfully employed nurse at St. Miguel Hospital. I make seventy-thousand dollars a year, give or take."

"We make a lot of deals with folks with smaller incomes than yours. So what do you think about a down payment?"

"I'd need to make arrangements."

"How about two thousand? You're not married?"

"No, I'm not, and I may be able to swing it. Will you need the hospital to validate my statements?"

"That would help."

"I should be able to get back to you in a week or so, maybe less if you're here on weekends. You are on commission, aren't you?"

"We are. I'm not married either, by the way."

"I'll get in touch with you shortly. Don't you dare sell that car to anybody else!"

"I shall guard it with my very life! Here's my card, complete with name, rank, and serial number."

As she walked out of the building, May thought, *Handsome and charming.*

Chapter Seven

May read that there was to be a large celebration after a Saturday soccer match at Jacksonville University. Wallace Tenor might be there. *Might as well scope out the territory at least, or I might get lucky,* she thought.

JU won the match. The proposed party was to go on even if they lost. Winning should enhance things. Of course, there would be no alcoholic beverages allowed—*nod, nod, wink, wink.*

That morning, May went to the Ford location and consummated the purchase of the new car. She had scraped together the three-thousand-dollar down payment. She hoped there would be no surprises.

Matt leaped to his feet when he spied her.

"Ms. May! Welcome back!"

"You haven't sold 'my' car, have you?"

"No. It's been under armed guard since you left."

"Good. I'd hate to have to court-martial you for dereliction of duty."

"You doing all right?"

"Fine. What do we do about my old car?"

"I'll have our man look it over and find out."

"When would we be doing that?"

Matt called out, "Steve! I need another estimate!"

Steve responded, "I live to serve. Where's the patient?"

After introductions, May took him to her old car.

"Looks better than most her age," Steve said.

May handed him her keys, and he moved it a short distance. He looked under the hood and in the trunk, and then he got on his knees to view the tires.

"Runs well?"

"Yes, sir."

"Why you selling it?"

"I'm afraid it'll quit doing so."

"Fifteen hundred. Sorry, it can't be more."

Since she expected only a thousand, she was more than satisfied.

"That's fine."

They returned to the building, and Matt escorted her to an office. "Have a seat, and I'll check with my slave master."

He was gone about five minutes.

"Thirty-nine minus fifteen hundred leaves thirty-seven five. How does that grab you?"

"I thought it started at forty thousand?"

"It did, but I arm-wrestled him down a notch."

"Okay, where do I sign?"

"In our manager's office. It's fancier than ours. Rank hath its privileges, you know."

The manager was cordial and efficient. No surprises—yet.

"We offer an extended warranty at a nominal price."

"Doesn't a three-year warranty come with it?"

"Yes. I mean after that."

"I read somewhere—do you know where you'll be in three years?"

"I guess I don't know for sure."

"Punch line—me neither."

"You got me there. Don't tell anybody I said so."

Monthly payments were reasonable as was the concurrent interest. Soon all were signed, sealed, and delivered.

"Matt'll take you to your new car. Good luck."

"One last question—I thought the base line was forty thousand?"

"It was till Matt forfeited his commission."

Out by the new car, Matt stated, "Well, here she is, all yours."

"He told me you negated your commission," May said.

"Well, I'm independently wealthy. I scoff at money."

"You won't get away with this! You'll be hearing from me!"

"Nothing would please me more."

CHAPTER EIGHT

May had no direct ties to JU that would facilitate an unobtrusive participation in the festivities. She was youthfully appearing, so she could readily pass as a student.

She drove her new car to JU and found a parking place in the public area. As she went farther on to the campus, the celebration seemed to be coming more from their field house than from the soccer field. With hundreds of people involved, she doubted she would ever catch a glimpse of Wally. She entered into the thick of things and accepted a glass of punch. She couldn't help but recall the doctored swigs of "punch" she had consumed before her assault. She didn't dwell on it nor did her pulse rate increase. She repressed the whole matter except for the off chance that Wally, by some miracle, would appear.

She carried on brief conversations with random students. A small sandwich or two, she accepted.

Suddenly, as if scripted, Wally was in plain view! Not only that, he was heading straight toward her. *Straight* might not be quite correct. He was wobbling noticeably, and he was homed in on her. She stood her ground. Now her pulse rate had increased!

"May! I need to talk with you—I need to apologize to you. Please hear me out." His words were a bit slurred, but he sounded sincere enough. "We can't talk in here. Come with me till we find some quiet place."

Since she had one hand on her mace cartridge, May agreed.

They ended up at the vacated stadium. Wally ascended the steps till they were at the top and then sat down. She sat down too, but not too close to him.

"May, I've felt terrible about what we did to you."

"Me too."

"It wasn't my idea, but I did participate. Can you ever forgive me?" He sounded sincere even through his alcohol fog.

"What do the other three think?"

"I don't communicate with any of them. I don't know."

She could ask him to stand up, and she could likely successfully shove him off the high stadium back. Why didn't she do it?

"I don't know how to make amends," Wally said.

She almost felt sorry for him. He was crying, rather harder than alcohol might induce.

He suddenly gave out a shriek, climbed the little barricade, and jumped off the bleachers. Other than for the hollow thud, there wasn't a sound.

CHAPTER NINE

What to do? May rushed down the steps and went to the back of the stadium. There he was! His body was contorted, and in the dim light, he didn't seem to be breathing. She called out for help, but with the party noise, there was no one to hear her. She ran back to the field house and spied a guard.

She rushed up to him and shouted above the din that someone had fallen off the stadium top. He ran back with her, and Wally was right where she'd left him. The guard felt for a pulse as he tried to see if the man was breathing. He could confirm neither. He straightened the body out. There were still no signs of life.

He pulled out his cell phone and dialed 911, both for an ambulance and the police. As they waited for the two, he asked her, "What happened?"

"We were just talking, and he suddenly screamed and jumped over the barricade and went over the ledge."

"Talking about what?"

"That's personal."

They were both quiet for the ten minutes it took the police to arrive. With the sirens blaring, the partygoers started to follow the noise. The ambulance wasn't far behind. It came more slowly to the location because of all the people walking on the road.

The police ascertained that the man was dead. They didn't try CPR, which would have been unavailing. The EMTs were of a like mind.

She gave the police the same answers to the same questions the guard had asked.

"What were you talking about?" the police asked.

"That's personal," May answered.

"Not with a dead man here! What was it?"

"He was apologizing to me."

"For what?"

"For raping me several years ago. That satisfy you?"

"Yes, it does. Sorry to have to ask about things, but I have to."

The EMTs took Wally's body away. The two cops reviewed the scene. They concluded that this one-hundred-twenty-pound girl couldn't have picked the two-hundred-pound man up and thrown him over the side.

The party was over—especially for Wallace B. Tenor.

CHAPTER TEN

The police had asked May to stay for a few minutes because their homicide detective, Lt. Buddy Short, was on his way and wanted to talk to her. She didn't mind doing so.

He came, and the policemen introduced them to each other. Buddy had a knack for interpreting people's testimony as to their veracity or lack thereof.

"Thank you for waiting, Ms. Stover. I won't take much of your time. I don't want to seem indelicate, but I do have to ask a few questions."

"Ask away."

"I was told that the deceased man had raped you a few years back."

"He and three others."

"I believe the four of them went to trial and were acquitted."

"Yes."

"How did you happen to run into him today?"

"I came looking for him."

"To what purpose?"

"To see if I wanted to kill him."

"But you didn't."

"No, he did that all by himself. He was drunk and tearfully remorseful about his part. I didn't tell him it was all right because it wasn't. In the middle of his seeking forgiveness, he suddenly screamed, ran to the edge, and threw himself over. The only sound after that was a thud. I ran down, and he was not breathing. He was dead. I yelled for help, but the festivities were so loud no one could hear me. I ran up to the party area and found a guard. He dialed 911 after confirming that Wallace was dead."

"Are you strong enough to have pushed him over the ledge?"

"I doubt it. If you have any other concern about me, I insist I be given a polygraph test here and now."

"That won't be necessary. How do you feel about all this?"

"Mixed feelings. I'm surprised how sad this makes me feel."

"I'm not. There's a world of difference between wishing someone were dead and seeing to it that it occurs. You're free to leave whenever you want to. Just leave your address and phone number for our records. I don't anticipate you'll be hearing from us again."

Chapter Eleven

May went directly home to her apartment. Wasn't this what she had wanted—what she had fantasized about? Like Scarlet, she decided she'd worry about it all tomorrow.

She went to work the next day. Wallace's death had made the eleven-o'clock television news, but her name was conspicuously absent. Or so her friend Janice told her.

"Wasn't that guy on your short list?"

"How did you know that?"

"You sort of told me when we were at dinner together."

"I did?"

"Wallace and the others."

"And you inferred that just from one word?"

"I'm ever so clever at keeping secrets too."

"I think it will be top news for a few days, and I was there when it happened. I'm prepared to give terse answers to nosy people."

"To mundane matters, how do you like the new car?"

"Love it! I found a new thingy I didn't know about. I changed lanes abruptly, and the car admonished me. I apologized, and we went along home."

"Have you named the little beauty yet?"

"No. Do you have any ideas?"

"I always fancied 'Janice,' but that could create confusion. How about 'Lone Ranger'? He rode a white horse."

"Mine's an off-white."

"If you were working in a savings-and-loan establishment, you could make it the Loan Arranger. How does that grab you?"

"Back-to-work time. Stay healthy."

"One last question, you going to call that car salesman?"

"Sometime soon—I'm off tomorrow."

CHAPTER TWELVE

May found herself with a day off, so she decided to give her car salesman, Matt Heller, a call. She couldn't let his declining his commission on her new car go unrewarded. Besides, she liked the cut of his jib, which had rarely happened for her since her trauma.

"Mr. Heller, May Stover here. Remember me?"

"It's Matt, if you please, and how could I ever forget the Mona Lisa, the pyramids, and you?"

"Did you know that the pyramids are five sided? You're not inferring—?"

"How about I change that to the Hanging Gardens of Babylon?"

"Better. Can you have lunch with me today? And I pay for it, without protest from you."

"Anything on the menu?"

"Anything your little heart desires."

"Yes, I can, at a place of your choosing."

"How about LongHorns on Southside Boulevard?"

"Love to. What time?"

"You set it. I'm off today."

"How about high noon but without Gary Cooper?"

"It'll hurt his feelings, but he'll get over it."

"I'd hoped you'd call."

"I'd hoped you'd hope I'd call."

"Is this what they call a date?"

"Yes, but don't call my mother."

As she turned off her cell phone, May felt a foreign tingle in her chest. Foreign because it would be her first real date since her trauma. If she had any misgivings, she didn't feel them.

Chapter Thirteen

Don Barney came home for his friend's funeral. The news from Wally's family was short and to the point. "Short illness" was short for "suicide." They just knew this was somehow that Stover girl's fault. May made a point of not attending the funeral.

Don understood that May had been around Wally when he jumped off the bleachers. She was too small to have had anything to do with his physical jumping. Wally had been the most remorseful of the four offenders. In retrospect, Don understood the psychology of it all. He himself carried no such burdens.

Though May did not attend the funeral service, she did make a point of slowly driving past the church just to see if any of the other three had attended. The church service ended, and out came the people, among whom was Don Barney.

May was becoming adept at hacking unobtrusively into the high school's records. Don's family home was not far from the small apartment May occupied. She had not given up her wish for revenge.

The date with Matt went well. He went back to work, and May went about her business, which included driving by the Barney home at dusk. She parked nearby and waited.

After half an hour, Barney drove up in his car and parked near his home. As May was speculating on how to harm him, a large man erupted from the nearby bushes and blindsided Don with the old sucker punch. He fell on top of his victim and continued to pummel him viciously.

May hesitated only briefly before leaping out of her car with her purse gun (minus the silencer) in her hand and screaming at the man. He clumsily got up and saw May. Don was unconscious.

"Get out of here, bitch!" he shouted, trotting toward her.

"Keep coming and I'll shoot you!" May shouted back.

"The hell you will!" he wheezed.

He was three feet from her when she fired two shots into his chest.

This was an interesting example of velocity and double motion. If he had been standing still, he would have gone over backward. As he was coming forward, he made two terminal steps before falling where May had been standing. Toreador.

She dialed 911 as she ran to Don's side. He was beginning to stir.

That guy might have killed him. Why did I intervene? May thought.

She ran to the door and called Don's parents out. You could hear sirens.

Don was sitting up now. His mother rushed out and screamed at May, "What have you done to him?"

"Just saved his life from that dead man over there," May said, pointing.

"Who's he?" Don's father asked.

"The jealous boyfriend of a girl I've been seeing," Don replied.

"Damn it, Don! You've got to clean up your act! Do you really want to be a doctor, or do you just want to party?" his father said loudly.

The squad cars pulled up right about then. May told them what had happened from her standpoint. Don was standing unsteadily by then. He was rubbing his jaw and his neck. The cop saw that not only did he have a broken jaw but also that his neck was bruised and he was hoarse.

"He was planning to kill you, you know," the cop said.

Chapter Fourteen

The police asked May to stay around till their lieutenant arrived. She understood that. Don was on his way to the hospital in the ambulance, and the few neighbors who had satisfied their curiosity had gone back to their homes.

Buddy Short arrived. They didn't know who was the more surprised at their meeting—May or Buddy.

"Ms. Stover, how do you explain this?"

"I can't."

"You seem to be a magnet for trauma. How did you happen to be here at the right time?"

May was hesitant. "I came by to see if Don was home."

"And if he had been and was uninjured, what were you going to do?"

"Leave and go home."

"I assume he was one of your attackers?"

"Yes."

"Do you routinely carry your gun?"

"Yes, I do." With that, May fished out her concealed weapon permit and handed it to Buddy.

He gave it a cursory glance and handed it back to her. "Had you considered shooting Don?"

"Yes."

"So instead of shooting him, you save his life."

"That's about it. Shoot him sometime—not here. Fantasizing."

"Should I inform the other two you're on the prowl?"

"I do plan to see them sometime."

"I know we're jesting, but don't do something foolish and ruin your own life."

"Thanks for caring."

Don's jaws would be wired shut for six weeks. His neck bruises were even more evident then. There was no doubt that his attacker had been out to kill him and that May Stover had saved his life. Buddy couldn't make sense of it all. Neither could May.

CHAPTER FIFTEEN

The dead fat man was sent to the morgue. They would not find a next of kin. His spartan apartment added nothing to his identity. He had a pay stub in his pocket that led the authorities to find out that he was an old-fashioned bouncer at a local bar. He was another potter's field applicant.

Don was able to give them the name of the girl who was presumed to be the basis for the assault. Contacting her, she was neither upset nor overly concerned. She'd only let the bouncer think he was her boyfriend to get free drinks, she told the police, as she avidly chewed her gum. The final report had a personal observation by the policeman: "Wearing excessive makeup."

Don was held over at the hospital because of his concussion. His wired jaws would give him six weeks of exposure to fortified drinks while he lost ten pounds. He was feeling pretty good for a fellow who had just narrowly escaped death.

May felt compelled to visit him again after work, on his second day in the hospital. He was very glad to see her and gave her a crooked smile.

"You do look abused," she said.

"Not nearly as abused as I would have been without your intercession." With his jaws wired shut, his speech was altered, but she understood him.

"When do you graduate from here?"

"Couple of days. I can return to school right away. You do know that if you save somebody's life, you're responsible for him ever after?"

"No, I didn't."

"Oh yes, it's widely known. I'm sorry. I know you can't like me very much—I don't like me very much either. I'll make it up to you sometime, somehow."

"Could I have that in writing?"

"Please don't make me laugh." Don grimaced.

"Was your little lady worth all this?"

"Sweet, but not that sweet."

Speaking of the devil, Ms. Spicer came in just then.

"Hey, honey, you look like hell," she said to Don.

"Glad to see you too. This is May Stover. She's the one that killed your bouncer," Don replied.

"Not my bouncer! That tub of lard got me free drinks, and that's all."

"We all grieve in our own way," Don said.

That went over Pam's head. May just shook her own head.

"Wow! So you really shot him, huh?" Pam asked May.

"I did." May could think of nothing further to add to that.

Pam had a pretty face with entirely too much makeup on it. She was also still avidly chewing some gum.

It was starting to seem like old home week. In walked Don's mother.

She knew who May was and assumed the other girl was at the root of her son's injuries. It required all her restraint to not show her anger.

"This is Pam Spicer, Mom," Don said.

She could not bring herself to say "Pleased to meet you." She was barely able to offer her hand to shake.

"He looks a lot like you," Pam said. She got half a point for that.

"Ms. Stover, I want to offer you my abject apology for my behavior at my home. I'm afraid I let my maternal part get entirely out of hand," Don's mother said, speaking to May.

"Understood. It's okay," May replied.

Don's mom swallowed. "You still got that gun?"

"No, the police have it temporarily."

Don's mom got a worried look on her face. "You doing all right, Don?"

"I'm fine, Mom. The warden says I'll be released tomorrow."

"Gotta go. I got a job interview to get to," Pam said suddenly. She gave Don a peck on the cheek and then sashayed out of the room.

"Job interview in the evening?" Mrs. Barney asked.

"She is a little ditsy."

"A little? What could you possibly have seen in her?"

May knew, and Don's mother really did too.

Chapter Sixteen

Six o'clock, Friday afternoon

"Hi, May. This is your favorite car salesman, Matt. How are you?"

"Hello there! I'm fine. How about you?"

"Lonesome. I sold three cars today, and here I am—nobody with which to celebrate."

"You poor dear. I suppose you've not had your evening nourishment either?"

"You know me like a book. I'm getting hungrier and hungrier by the minute."

"And you hate to dine alone, right?"

"There's that book again. Do you happen to know of anyone who would have dinner with me on short notice this evening?"

"I'll bet I can find a volunteer."

"I would pay for both dinners, of course, providing the other party stayed on the first page of the menu."

"That's a given."

"May I, Ms. May, pick you up in thirty minutes?"

"Great. That will give me time to put my gourmet food back in the freezer."

Matt arrived thirty minutes later on the dot.

"You look ravishing, as usual," he said to May.

"And you, Adonis reincarnated."

"A what?"

"You know, Persephone's hottie."

"Oh, that one. Wasn't he killed by a boar?"

"Sort of. Zeus gave him a second chance."

"I will certainly be on the lookout for any boars."

"LongHorns okay again?"

"Long, short, any old way."

May had her salmon while Matt had a Flo's Filet. They cleaned their plates during their animated conversation.

Damn, he is handsome! she thought.

Damn, she is beautiful! he thought.

CHAPTER SEVENTEEN

Eight-thirty, back to May's apartment

"Matt, I've had a lovely evening, but I'm not ready to invite you in yet, okay?" May said.

"I'm not ready to ask to come in. It's okay," Matt replied.

They hugged then separated.

May knew the feelings! She hadn't had them since her assault. She sure did have them now! A cold shower was needed, maybe?

She gave that about one second and then dodged till the hot water kicked in.

Meanwhile, Matt was dealing with his own hormones. They both slept the sleep of the innocent that night, dreaming they were guilty.

CHAPTER EIGHTEEN

Don had ample opportunities to perfect his response to inquiries about his black-and-blue face and his wired jaws. They included "None of your business!" "You should see the other guy," "This girl was a martial-arts instructor," etc.

Somehow, most everybody in Gainesville hadn't heard of his escapade. He'd leak it out bit by bit. He'd lost five pounds already. It took a lot of grit to get back to studying. There wouldn't be many "poor babies" for him in medical school.

He tried to repress his guilty feelings about May. Having a lady save your life after you have majorly wronged her jams the circuits. He would make it up to her somehow, sometime. He didn't waste any time worrying about the troll May shot.

Chapter Nineteen

Two weeks after the obese man who May had fatally shot was buried in Jacksonville's version of a potter's field, his brother, Luigi Silencia, showed up. He checked out the last place his sibling had lived. The apartment was empty. On asking the manager about things, he got the main points of his brother's demise.

"So he was trying to kill a man he thought was messing with his girlfriend?"

"Right."

"A woman saw what was happening and shot him dead?"

"Right."

"This other woman—you said she was in a car—do you know why she was where she was then?"

"Nope."

"He's buried already?"

"Right."

"The police didn't charge the lady?"

"Course not. Your brother would have killed the guy if she hadn't shot him. Oh, the paper said she called out, telling him to stop, and he got up and came after her—that's where he got himself shot."

"Thank you for the information. Did he owe you any money?"

"Nope. Paid his rent in cash every month. You don't look like him. He was three hundred pounds if he was an ounce, and you're what? One forty?"

"We ate differently. Have you rented his apartment yet?"

"Nope."

"How much would it be for one month as is?"

"Four hundred—that's what he paid."

"Where's his stuff?"

"Downstairs in the basement."

"Put back what you think I'd need here, and I'll give you a hundred dollars."

"Will do."

With that, Luigi pulled out a roll of hundreds that really would choke a horse. He peeled off six and handed them to the manager.

"Did he have a cell phone?"

"Think so. Didn't run into it up here."

Luigi needed access to his late brother's personal effects. They would be in police custody. He called his home office and asked them to FedEx him paper copies showing his relationship to his brother.

As he was having dinner and before returning to his new temporary apartment, Luigi mused over how such a happening would have been dealt with in Sicily. The girl would probably be eliminated.

Chapter Twenty

Luigi had been using Uber in Jacksonville, much as he routinely did in New York City. He decided to rent a car and ended up with a current off-white Ford.

First, he called the police department and, after talking to the fourth person, was put through to Buddy Short, whose name was on the papers attendant to Guido Silencia's death.

"Mr. Silencia, there were no papers in his apartment that alluded to you or anybody else other than his employer. His employer knew nothing about his family or friends. I presume you know what led to his death?"

"I heard a sketchy version from his landlord. Could you amplify for me?"

"He had a sometime girlfriend who also dated a young man who's in medical school. Your brother looked him up and was busy trying to kill him when another young lady happened by and ordered him to stop. He stopped but came after her. She had a licensed gun and shot him."

"How were you sure he was trying to kill the man?"

"The man had bruises on his neck, which you get from a strangulation attempt. Besides, he came after the lady. Your brother was a violent man, sir."

"It would seem so. He's already buried?"

"Yes, he is."

"What about his personal effects?"

"We have them. If you have documentation, we can turn them over to you."

"I do. Where should I go?"

"Police Memorial Building. Anytime from eight to five."

"Thank you for being patient with me. He was always a maverick, but he was my brother."

"I understand."

After Buddy closed the phone connection, he reflected on the conversation. He didn't like the guy. He couldn't explain to himself why that was so. Should he contact Ms. Stover? It wouldn't hurt to.

"Ms. Stover, Buddy Short. I just had a conversation with Guido's brother," Buddy said as soon as his call connected.

"I thought he had no family," May replied.

"Seems he does."

"Why did you call me about it?"

"If they were Sicilian, they take family honor seriously."

"Good God! You don't mean—"

"I just had bad vibes talking to him. Thought you needed to know."

Chapter Twenty-One

If there was any kind of a threat to May, there would be an even bigger one to Don Barney. She had no trouble getting his phone number from his mother. No, nothing was wrong (yet).

"Don, May here. How's it going?"

"Not too bad. Yourself?"

"Fine."

She relayed Buddy's impressions to him.

"You mean this brother could be a threat to both of us?"

"Obviously, not for sure. Just possible."

"You're making a habit of trying to save my life."

"I feel a little silly now that I think about it."

"I'm all for an ounce of prevention. I do thank you, and I'll go to yellow alert for now."

"Should I call Pam Spicer?"

"I'll take care of that."

Back at Don's parents' home, April (Don's mother) was speaking to her husband, who had just arrived home.

"That Stover girl called me to get Don's phone number. I think she may be getting sweet on him."

"April, you're a hopeless romantic."

"Well, it's possible. Don't you recall how they met? The only difference between rape and seduction is salesmanship."

"Good heavens, April! I never heard you talk like that!"

"Do you have anything you'd care to sell me?"

Chapter Twenty-Two

The job interview didn't go well, and Pam didn't get it. Well, she didn't want it anyway. Back at the bar where her late sometime boyfriend worked, Pam Spicer nursed a drink till somebody else offered to buy her another one.

Thin, rather handsome, and with a radiant smile, the new patron offered to buy her a drink.

"Did you know the bouncer that used to work here?"

"Sure. I used to date him. You knew him?"

"I'm his brother."

"You're puttin' me on!"

"No, I came down to settle his estate. He spoke of you often."

"He never mentioned you or any other relative."

"He was a shy child."

"Boy, he wasn't shy here. I saw him pick up a two-hundred-pound rowdy and throw him out in the street. He could crush a beer can with his hands too."

"Yes, he was very strong as a child. He didn't do all that well in school though."

"He must have gotten your food too, growin' up. You don't look anything like him!"

"I heard he attacked some medical student."

"He sure did. Was tryin' to kill him!"

"Why would he do a thing like that?"

"As I said, I used to date him some—nothin' full-time. I had a couple of dates with this med student, and Guido got mad about it."

"Some lady shot him, I heard."

"She just happened by, and he went after her, they said,"

"Do you work here?"

"Naw, just hangin' out. I'm between jobs right now."

"Care for another drink?"

"I believe I would, thank you."

Luigi nursed his drink as Pam had one and then another. She was a pretty little thing, he thought. Pretty and soused.

"You live near here?" he asked her.

"Jus' down the street," she answered in a slurred voice.

"Why don't I see you safely home?"

She nodded, either affirmatively or sleepily or both.

Luigi had to fish through her purse for her apartment key. By this time, she was staggering and about to fall down.

Her bedroom was the only other room in her apartment, so he ushered her in. She was essentially asleep by then. He found a set of pajamas and took her clothes off.

He left a memento for her, for services rendered. She found two hundred-dollar bills on her dresser top. It would have cost him five hundred back in New York.

CHAPTER TWENTY-THREE

"Pam, Don Barney. Are you all right?"

"Hi there! I have a bit of a headache, but otherwise I'm okay."

"Allergy from what you consumed at the bar?"

"Something like that."

"You need to know that Guido has a brother, and he came to town a day or two ago."

"Yeah, met him last night! Nice guy."

"This 'nice guy' is probably from a Sicilian family. They take a dim view of people that kill their relatives."

"I didn't kill nobody."

"Not directly, but you were involved."

"I was, wasn't I?"

"You more than just met him?"

"Yeah, you could say that."

"Well, I just wanted you to know how things could be."

"Thanks. We got along fine. In fact, he left me two-hundred dollars."

"Out of the goodness of his heart?"

Pam snickered. "That would be anatomically incorrect. You didn't know I knew them big words, did you?"

"No. Just be alert."

"We gonna be seein' each other anytime soon?"

"Probably not. I have to work all the harder, what with my broken jaw."

"Guido never laid a hand on me."

"He did on me."

Chapter Twenty-Four

A call was sent out to New York City. "Father, I plan to stay in Jacksonville for a couple of weeks to get this all sorted out."

"Guido, did your brother die nobly?"

"Not especially. He was attacking a lady, and she shot him."

"Why was he attacking her?"

"She interrupted him when he was trying to kill a man."

"And why was that?"

"A young girl was Guido's sometime girlfriend. She also dated a medical student. Guido was attempting to eliminate the competition."

"So headstrong. Was he still fat?"

"Even fatter, from what I have been told."

"So who pays?"

"The med student for sure. The other woman maybe. How do you see it?"

"Firstly, I don't want you to get into any trouble in any of your actions. I've already lost one son. Use the utmost discretion. That other woman is beside the point, it seems to me."

"Absolutely, as to the discretion part. How is Mother?"

"Fine. Always stewing over you."

"And the business?"

"Thriving. Since our phone could be tapped, I'll not elaborate."

"Will you be going back to Sicily this year?"

"Maybe not. This cough of mine is tiresome."

"What does the doctor say?"

"Haven't seen one yet."

"Why?"

"Struthious."

"And that means what?"

"'Of or pertaining to the ostrich.' Head-in-the-sand stuff."

"Was that your new word for the day?"

"Sure, why not?"

Chapter Twenty-Five

"May, this is your friendly neighborhood car salesman. How are you?"

"Fine. And you?"

"A trifle lonesome."

"Only a trifle?"

"Well, a big trifle. Are you available for dinner this evening?"

"I believe I can work that into my tight social schedule."

"Great. Six o'clock work?"

"Like a charm."

When they met, May and Matt hugged, and then they went to Matt's car.

"I'll wait till we get seated to discuss something." May said.

"A hint?"

"Has to do with the family of the man I shot."

"Have you noticed how respectful I've become since I learned you were packin'?"

"Yes, I've been wondering about that. I have reloaded, by the way."

"Sold three more cars today."

"Wonderful! You up for any awards?"

"Probably, but I was looking for more money."

"My head nurse told me if I needed more money, go to any bank. They have loads of it."

"Okay—what's the mystery?"

"We were all told that the Guido guy I shot didn't have any family. His brother showed up in Jacksonville two days ago."

"Have you met him?"

"No, and I don't care to. The police lieutenant I met called me about the guy and wanted me to pay attention to my surroundings."

"Vendetta crap?"

"Only possible. I do have that concealed weapon, and I recently cleaned it."

"So won't that medical student be in a lot more jeopardy than you?"

"I would think so."

"Why don't we order some food and see if we can find another subject to explore."

"I like my hospital and my boss. Can't beat that with a stick."

"I like my boss too, and he likes me too. I think that's because of my scintillating personality and not the bunch of cars I've sold."

"He's also likely impressed with your modesty."

The food came. It was good.

"There's something I need to tell you," May said suddenly.

Matt knew the mood had abruptly changed. "Okay, shoot. Oops, wrong word. Lay it on me."

"When I was seventeen, I was gang-raped by four classmates. I allowed them to get me drunk for the first and only time in my life. They were exonerated because I didn't have any bruises."

"You poor kid."

"That comes to two other items. One was I planned to kill them all."

"You're serious?"

"I was. The first one jumped off the stadium's backside and killed himself right in front of me."

"How did that make you feel?"

"Terrible. I felt no satisfaction at all."

"I take it that med student was number two?"

"Yes. I'm considering cold-blooded murder, and I end up saving his life."

"That would cloud the issue. What's number two?"

"I'm not sure I can perform a marital act."

"I'm in no hurry for anything. We can just be friends. That way you'll feel obligated to buy all your cars from me."

May was on the verge of tears. "I'm a mess, aren't I?"

"Anything but. We can leave things like they are for now."

"You're so sweet and understanding. I think I love you."

"And I know I love you."

The evening ended with more hugs—perhaps a little longer and a bit tighter.

CHAPTER TWENTY-SIX

May contacted her friend, Janis Barkely, asking if she were available for dinner one evening that week. Janis worked in the same hospital as May but in a different section.

"How was your day, Janis?"

"Moderately hectic. How about you?"

"Not too bad. What are you going to order?"

"Salmon, I guess."

"Me too. Are we having a glass of wine?"

"Why not a glass for each of us?"

"Brilliant!"

May had never consumed more than one glass of wine per evening since her trauma.

"So how's your love life?"

"I'm getting fonder and fonder of my car salesman. How about you?"

"There's a new young nurse on the floor adjacent to mine that has the wings. Don't know if she flies. Anything affecting your med student?"

"Yes. Guido's brother showed up in town a few days ago."

"I thought he didn't have any relatives."

"So did we."

"Is he causing any trouble?"

"Not yet, but he's Sicilian. Lieutenant Short told me to be cautious."

"What's he going to do about it?"

"Nothing. The guy's got a right to be here."

"Don't Sicilians take a dim view of relatives being killed?"

"I believe that's true. Don Barney should be even more alert."

"He knows all about this?"

"Yes."

"You're not getting sweet on him too, are you?"

"I don't think so, but saving his life is a game changer."

"Have you met Dr. Prince?"

"He's a general surgeon, isn't he? I've heard of him."

"His father is supposed to be Haitian. His skin color is beautiful, just like yours."

"Which one?"

"Both of them, I'm told."

"The OR nurses love him, I've heard."

"You need to see him sometime. Maybe you're related. They also say he's prescient about things."

"Prescient?"

"You know, sees things before they happen."

"Now I really want to meet him."

The next morning.

"Good morning, Ms. Stover. I understand you wanted to meet me, and I wanted to meet you too. I'm Dr. Prince."

Chapter Twenty-Seven

"You don't seem very surprised to see me," Dr. Prince said to May.

"I'm not, but I should be. Very happy to meet you, sir."

"Our skin colors are almost identical, aren't they?"

"I'm supposed to be 25 percent Latino—probably Mexican."

"My father is Haitian, but his skin color has lightened over the years to where he resembles us. Do you have visions of the future?"

"Not really, though I somehow knew you would be over this morning."

"You have a problem with a Sicilian."

"Where did you hear that?"

"Nowhere. I just know. He will not harm you. Your friend in Gainesville could go either way."

"This is just too weird!"

"You'll get used to it. It's an imperfect gift, but sometimes it can be lifesaving. I must be going. We'll talk again if you wish."

"I wish!"

May went back to the nurses' station and sat down to do some charting. Going digital hadn't replaced her job.

She wondered what the Sicilian was up to today. She concentrated hard. Nothing came.

CHAPTER TWENTY-EIGHT

Luigi couldn't get Pam out of his mind. She was such a sweet and trusting girl, and he had taken advantage of her. In his business, you took advantage of people before they took advantage of you. He was unfamiliar with the emotion he was now sensing—remorse.

In his rental car, he drove to Pam's apartment, on the off chance she might be there. She was.

"Well, hi there. Didn't expect we'd see each other today," Pam said to Luigi.

"Neither did I. May I come in?"

"Of course. Care for a Coke or something else?"

"That would be nice. I'm glad you look as perky as you do. You were a bit wasted last evening."

"You think so? I only had one drink."

"What did you do with the other three you ordered?"

"Oh them? What I usually do. Poured them into the potted plant behind the table."

Luigi was stunned! He looked at her intently. "Where's the gum?"

"I don't really like to chew it."

Pam had a modest amount of makeup on. She looked beautiful!

"Run out of make up?" Luigi asked.

"Oh that—camouflage. This is the real me."

"I'm about as close to being bewildered as I've ever been," Luigi said.

Pam smiled. "I'm not really that ditsy either."

"I can see that. Why . . . why—"

"Because I wanted to. I singled you out because I thought you were dangerous."

"Other people think I am too."

"You're gentle, thoughtful, and kind, so get over it—oh, and generous too."

"Who are you really?"

"I have a graduate degree in English. My parents are deceased. I'm not rich, but they left me enough that I don't have to work if I don't want to. My IQ is 142, give or take. I don't give myself easily, including to your brother. He was my protector, and that was all. He obviously thought that medical student was all wrong for me. I do too. Heard enough?"

"I really liked you the way you were last night. Now I love you the way you are today, or something like that."

"I'm a real vamp, aren't I?"

"About last night—"

"Very pleasurable, and you were ever so gentle putting my PJs on me. You know what really brought tears to my eyes? When you kissed me sweetly on my cheek, just before you left."

"How about some lunch?"

"Good idea. There's a little restaurant just down the street. Not gourmet but neither am I."

Luigi had a hard time taking his eyes off of Pam there.

CHAPTER TWENTY-NINE

May thought off and on about what Dr. Prince had told her. She couldn't quite accept that she might be prescient. She hadn't been up till then. He had said that the visions would come on their own. You couldn't bring them up on demand.

Two days after her conversation with Dr. Prince, May was on her morning coffee break in the nurses' lounge with a fellow nurse. They were chitchatting about inconsequential things when May had a vivid image that one of her patients in room 202 had just sustained a cardiac arrest!

She leaped to her feet and ran to the room. The monitoring devices seemed to be working, but the patient's EKG showed he was in ventricular fibrillation! She pushed the room button and screamed as she began CPR on the unconscious man.

Moments later, professionals were hurrying to the room, crash cart in tow. Electrodes were applied to the man's chest. Contact with his body was interrupted.

Zap! The man twitched, but the EKG was unchanged. The voltage was increased, and the process repeated. A regular pulse! By this time, the man had an endotracheal tube in place, with oxygen being administered.

He now had a life-sustaining blood pressure level. He was beginning to move on his own, opening and closing his eyes. He was bucking on his tube, and with his coming around so well, he was extubated.

As the tube came out, he could then voice, "What the hell was that in my throat?" Such patients as this weren't usually that rapidly rendered conscious. He was. It was a very good sign.

His admitting physician was alerted, and he came as fast as he could to the room.

"Hey, Doc, what the hell happened here?" the patient asked.

"You tried to die, but the folks here wouldn't let you. We keep you monitored, and that's what saved you."

The nurses knew that the monitors had somehow failed to activate and that May Stover had been the one to alert them.

Crisis being over, May tried to explain how she knew about the event. The more she tried, the more everyone was mystified. Personnel went back to DEFCON.

The nurse who was with May in the lounge would tell her story, and that would generate askance looks and little else. The malfunction in the monitor system was quietly corrected. Nobody wanted to talk about that.

May tried to suppress her elation. She could hardly wait to see Dr. Prince again.

Chapter Thirty

The restaurant they went to was close enough for a walk. It was a beautiful morning, and Pam and Luigi were in high spirits.

"Does everybody call you Luigi?" Pam asked.

"No. Actually, most people call me Lou."

"Well, I certainly want to be like most people, Lou."

"You are a lot of things, but being like most people is not one of them. I've never met anyone like you. That may explain my fascination with you."

"I'm fascinating?"

"That you are."

They picked a table off to the side, as private as the restaurant afforded. "Breakfast or lunch?"

"Maybe lunch. They make an outstanding Reuben here."

"If you have one, so will I."

"I usually can't finish mine, and so I take the rest home. Tell me about yourself, Lou." Pam looked at him intently.

"My father has an import business, and I work with him."

"What do you import?"

"Whatever there's a market for in New York. Art objects, for instance."

"What brought you down here? Guido was already buried, and he didn't have any assets."

"Both my father and I wanted to find out why he was killed."

"I can tell you that. He had this misguided notion that I needed protection. He took it on his own to beat up this med student I was casually dating. I guess he got carried away. He almost killed the guy."

"Did you know the lady who shot him?"

"No. She just happened by and confronted him. Your brother stopped trying to kill the man and came after her. He was 100 percent in the wrong."

"It looks like I came down here to meet you."

"You're awfully sweet for a dangerous man."

Chapter Thirty-One

Dr. Leon Prince showed up at the nurses' station where May worked, just as she had anticipated.

"Good morning, doctor. I've been expecting you."

"Oh, you have? I came over to compliment you for saving that patient's life yesterday."

"I was right here in this very room when I suddenly knew the man was in cardiac arrest—well, fibrillation actually."

"Now you see how your 'gift' can accomplish remarkable things."

The other nurse who had been with May when she had her vision happened in on the two of them. "Oh, sorry. I'll come back later," she said.

"No, please stay. We were just discussing that cardiac arrest case yesterday. Were you in on the resuscitation?" Dr. Prince asked.

"Yes, sir. I pushed the crash cart in, among other things."

"All of you did your job, and the gentleman would be dead if you hadn't."

"Did you did there was a malfunction in the alarm system?"

Dr. Prince said, smiling, "It's being downplayed and rectified."

"We don't understand how May knew about the arrest, but she was out of the lounge like she was shot out of a cannon when she somehow knew what was happening."

"It's called premonition. Our little May here seems to be gifted that way," Dr. Prince said.

"Am I getting a raise anytime soon?" the other nurse asked.

Dr. Prince smiled, "Define *soon*."

"Oh, you know—sometime before Christmas."

"Madam May sees a raise in your future and a new boyfriend," May said.

"Will he be rich?"

"I'm sorry. The crystal ball has gotten cloudy."

"I must go. We'll talk again soon, if you wish," Dr. Prince said.

"I wish very much so," May replied.

Once Dr. Prince was out of earshot, the other nurse asked, "Are you two related? Your skin colors are identical."

"Not that I know of," May said.

"Why don't you get your DNA analyzed?"

"I may at that. No telling what might come up."

CHAPTER THIRTY-TWO

Sam Sales was in law school and doing very well. He was one of the four who had assaulted May Stover several years back. His folks had told him that Don had a broken jaw, so Sam called him.

"What's with the broken jaw, pilgrim?"

"You haven't heard the tale?"

"No, Mom just said you broke your jaw, so I'm calling to see if you need my counseling."

"Well, I didn't break my jaw, I had it broken for me. You really haven't heard the story?"

"No, but I'd sure like to."

"I'd been casually dating a girl named Pam Spicer, and she had a male friend who didn't think I was right for her."

"'Casually' meaning you hadn't scored?"

"Something like that. Anyway, I was visiting my folks one weekend, was heading up the steps at my folk's house, and this three-hundred-pound bozo blindsided me, breaking my jaw. He then started choking me. He was going to kill me."

"My God! Really? How did you get saved?"

"A lady was driving by and stopped her car. She had a gun and screamed at the man to stop."

"She had a gun?"

"Right. He got off me and ran at her."

"You're not putting me on, are you?"

"Nope. She ordered him to stop. He didn't. She shot him dead."

"Why was the lady there at all?"

"Possibly planning on shooting me."

"Now you're really spooking me out."

"She was maybe planning on shooting me but shot him instead."

"Whew! Did you know her?"

"Yes, and so do you."

"You're really enjoying dragging this out, aren't you?"

"Does the name May Stover ring a bell?"

"My God!"

"I wonder if you're on her visitation list too."

Chapter Thirty-Three

The ripening of her visions didn't impede May's growing love for Matt Heller.

They were at the stage of sustained kisses and caresses. She knew that she would soon have to try her wings or end the relationship.

They were having dinner together at May's apartment one evening. It was time to tell him about her visions. She hoped it wouldn't scare him off.

"Matt, I need to tell you something about myself."

"That you're adorable? I already knew that."

"Not exactly. Recently I've been having visions of things to come that do happen. Do you know Dr. Prince?"

"Sure. Sold him a car last year."

"Well, he has the same ability, and he knew that I was having these visions. The case I told you about where the patient had a cardiac arrest? Well, I sensed it before any monitor fired. I saved his life. The management played it down because their monitors had malfunctioned."

"That's okay. Virtue is its own reward. Do they always come to pass?"

"Dr. Prince says no, but the few I've had did occur."

"Have you had any of your visions about me?"

"Yes. I need to get something from my bedroom."

She was gone only a few minutes and returned wearing a thin dressing gown.

"You don't have to do this, you know," Matt said.

"Oh, yes, I do!"

Chapter Thirty-Four

6:00 AM

"Can't we both call in and tell them we've had a sinking spell and can't work today?"

"Great idea but, 'I could not love thee half so well, loved I not honor more.'"

"That's pretty heavy stuff. I have some fruit in the fridge if you want some."

They parted ways with a clear understanding that they loved one another.

"What are you humming about, May?" another nurse asked her.

"Just happy."

"Right. You getting heavy with that car salesman of yours?"

"Is it that obvious?"

"To the trained eye, like mine, yes."

May went back to work. At lunchtime there was a vision! Sam Sales! What? Violence in a bar! As quickly as it had come upon her, it left. May had to contact him! After work would be soon enough.

"Mrs. Barney, this is May Stover. Do you have Sam Sales's phone number?"

"No, I don't. Don would."

"Could you give it to me?"

"Surely."

Mrs. Barney wanted to know why May needed the number but was reluctant to ask.

"I want to apologize again for my behavior just after Don's injury. I will be ever grateful that you saved my son's life."

"No apology needed. Thanks for the number," May said before hanging up.

"Sam?"

"Yes."

"This is May Stover. Are you planning on going to a bar this evening?"

Sam was totally confused. "Probably. Why?"

"I had this vision of violence there, and you would be at risk."

"What's this all about?"

"Sam, I had this vision, and you would be in great danger there."

"Vision?"

"I know. Sounds weird. Please, please do not go to the bar this evening!"

"Maybe I won't."

"No maybes about it! Please!"

To say that Sam was befuddled would be to put it mildly. What May said was never far out of his mind as the day progressed.

"Still going with me tonight?" his classmate asked.

"I'd better not. This corporate law stuff isn't too clear yet. Why don't we both not go?"

"And break the heart of Tiffany? I'm too honorable to do that."

His classmate went to his bar, and Sam went to his books. He was able to focus well enough to grasp the subject matter.

The next morning.

"Hey, did you hear about Bart?" a friend asked Sam.

"No. What about him?" Sam replied.

"He was shot at that bar he liked to go to."

"How is he?"

"He's dead."

CHAPTER THIRTY-FIVE

"Hey, Don. Do you have May Stover's phone number?"

"It should still be on my past calls. I'll check and call you right back."

"Hi. It's 904 4228777. What's up?" Don said.

"I had a classmate who was killed last night in a bar. I was going with him till May called me."

"Yeah, I gave her your number. She seemed anxious."

"She pleaded with me not to go. Something about violence."

"How would she know about that?"

"Something about a vision she had. She probably saved me from being shot too."

"Well, I guess we can rule out her coming for you with a weapon."

"We were so despicable with her, and she saves both of our lives."

"I went through that same thought pattern. We owe her. Big time."

"Take care. When do your jaws reopen?"

"Couple of weeks. I'm feeling fine. Losing some weight I didn't need anyway."

"May, this is Sam. I took your advice and avoided the bar. I guess you heard that my classmate was killed there last night," Sam said as May answered his call.

"Thank you for staying away from there," May replied.

"Thank me? You saved my life—it's I who should be doing the thanks. I was despicable with you, and then you save my life. I'm so sorry."

"That's okay. No permanent damage."

Sam wasn't quite sure what she meant by that, but he did know he would be ever in her debt.

CHAPTER THIRTY-SIX

Victor Post was another participant in the previous assault on May Stover. He'd kept in casual contact with his three friends who had also been involved. He had an educational degree and was teaching social studies at Episcopal High School.

He had heard that Wally Tenor had committed suicide right in front of May. It was unsettling. He next heard about Don Barney's close call, with May saving his life. He called Don and got the details.

"May just happened by in time to shoot your assailant?" Victor asked Don.

"Yes. She did."

"Why was she there in the first place?"

"Maybe to shoot me, but she saved my life instead."

"This sounds like fantasy. Do you find any logic here?"

"Not really. Did you hear about Sam?"

"I guess not. Haven't talked to him for a while."

"He was planning on going to a bar with a classmate one evening. He got a call from May. She had experienced some sort of a vision that indicated there would be violence there and he would be in grave danger."

"A vision?"

"Like a premonition. He finally elected to stay in his apartment and study. His classmate went ahead and was shot and killed at the bar."

"Good grief! I hadn't heard about that."

"It just happened very recently."

"This is all too weird. She must hate us, and yet she goes around saving our lives. Well, yours anyway. So I shouldn't be surprised if she shows up on my doorstep with a gun in one hand and a bandage in the other."

"I'd give odds you'll see her before long. How's teaching going?"

"I have a few students who thirst for knowledge, but most of them thirst for the closing bell."

"You mean like us when we were in school?"

"I've repressed it all. I've always been good at denial."

"Let me know when you hear from her."

"If I'm able to."

CHAPTER THIRTY-SEVEN

May would go days without a vision and then have two in a row. They weren't about life-threatening events so far, except for Sam.

She went up to some of the older nurses on the surgical floors, asking about Dr. Prince.

They all loved him. They would all want him for any surgical needs of their own. He was always courteous and appreciative of the hospital employees.

May had noticed that he was supposed to be in his early forties, but he looked more like he was in his early twenties. She'd seen his wife one time. She was pretty but looked to be in her early forties. They said he had two children, a girl who had milk-white skin and a boy who had the same color skin as his father.

The nurses said that Dr. Prince also knew when to decline to operate on someone. They remembered one case in particular—a patient who was too sick to survive surgery. One of the younger surgeons thought he could take care of things. He couldn't, and the patient died the day after surgery. It was a humbling experience.

One nurse had seen Dr. Prince's father. He was a Haitian, and his skin color was like his son's. Said to be seventy, he looked to be forty-five.

Several of the more-aggressive hospital employees would come up to May, asking if she could predict something or other about themselves. Her standard answer was that visions didn't come on demand, but if she had one involving them, she'd be sure to let them know.

The head nurse had come to resent all the attention May was receiving. She felt she should be getting the attention. She sent a message for May to come to her office. On her way there, May had a flash. It made her smile.

The head nurse began berating May, accusing her of drawing attention to herself, and if she didn't cease, she would fire her.

May just smiled through the tirade.

"And just what are you smiling about, young lady?" the head nurse asked May.

"You're being fired next week."

And she was.

Chapter Thirty-Eight

May's reveries about Matt were entirely different from her visions, which generally showed up unsolicited. If their relationship didn't change from what it was at the time, they would get married. They even hypothecated that two children would be quite enough.

A vision! It involved Vic Post, one of the four men who had assaulted her back in high school. He was lying on the floor somewhere. He was not moving. The vision faded out.

May knew the school where Vic worked, and she called it, asking for Vic's phone number. The clerk was resistant to giving it to her until May said it was an emergency. After giving the number, the clerk volunteered that Mr. Post had not come to school that day.

May dialed the number, and a man with a husky voice answered.

"I'm May Stover. I need to speak to Vic!"

"One moment" came the reply. That moment was the time to give the phone to Lieutenant Buddy Short. Buddy identified himself and asked her who she was.

"May Stover. We've met before. What's happened?"

"Mr. Post has died from a gunshot. We're not sure whether it was self-inflicted or not. I remember you. That suicide out at the university."

"I remember you also."

"May I ask why you were calling?"

Might as well tell it like it is, May thought. "I had a premonition something had happened to him."

"Wasn't he one of the four who assaulted you in high school?"

"Yes, he was." She knew where this was going.

"Were you on good terms with Vic?"

"I wasn't on any terms with him. I hadn't seen him since he left the courtroom smirking. And no, I didn't shoot him, and I'll be glad to give my gun to ballistics."

"You do know, we have to explore all the avenues."

"Of course. I'm not working today. Would you like me to come over there?"

"That would be nice."

"Then I'll need his address."

He gave it to her. He had almost ruled her out as the shooter at that time. Almost.

CHAPTER THIRTY-NINE

"A May Stover to see you. Said you were expecting her."
"Yes. Let her in, please."

"You look like you did when I met you. Thanks for coming," Lieutenant Buddy said to May as way of greeting.

"Could I see the body? I am a nurse, and I've seen a lot of bodies," May replied.

It wasn't exactly protocol, but he pulled the sheet back.

"That's him plus forty pounds or so," May said.

"Gained a lot of weight, had he?"

"Quite a bit. Here's my gun and permit. I took the bullets out. Do you want one to test?"

"No thanks. I believe we can round one up at headquarters. Did your premonition cast any light on what we have here?"

"No. I saw him in exactly the position he's in now. The added forty pounds didn't show."

"So you hadn't spoken to him recently?"

"Absolutely not. I've made peace with the other two men."

"I believe you saved the life of that med student and killed his assailant."

"That's right. I also headed the other one off before he went to a bar where his associate was killed."

"That was in Gainesville, wasn't it?"

"Yes."

"So your good deeds go beyond Jax?"

"It appears so."

CHAPTER FORTY

It was about time for Matt to get off work, so May drove to the automobile store. Matt's associates liked him and were well aware that things were getting serious with May.

"Hey, May, Wonder Boy is just finishing a sale. He'll be out shortly," they told May.

"No hurry," May replied.

"Are there anymore at home like you?"

"My parents are glad there weren't."

"He talks all the time about your myriad of good traits. I think you have him under your spell."

"Did he ever mention that I'm a witch?"

"No, but we already guessed that."

Matt came out of his office, shaking the hand of the proud new owner of a brand-new car. Seeing the connection between the two of them, the customer asked, "That your wife?"

"Not quite."

"Better close the deal, Matt." Three of Matt's associates were banded together and offered their rehearsed ballad. "Matt and May sittin' by the tree. K-i-s-s-i-n-g. First comes love. Then comes marriage. Then comes Matt with a baby carriage."

"I think all three of you need to keep your daytime jobs" was Matt's studied conclusion.

CHAPTER FORTY-ONE

"You're free to go, of course. We'll get your gun back to you in a couple of days. Thanks again for coming over."

"Which way are you betting?"

"Murder, probably. You don't know whether he was right- or left-handed, do you?"

"Underhanded, as best I know."

"Well, forensics corporation, thumbs up or down?"

"Probably murder. The angle of entry into the skull would be a strain for a right-handed person. It's hard to pull a trigger with your hand so compromised. Also, he has an injury to his scalp. Blunt object? Recent—like just before the bullet, for instance."

"Well done, good and faithful servants."

"We live to serve."

"Anybody home in the adjacent houses?" Buddy asked an officer.

"Slim pickings. It's a working neighborhood mostly. One lady two doors down heard nothing, saw nothing, and offered minimal information about the victim. Said he was not neighborly but no trouble whatsoever."

"Sound sleeper?"

"I asked her. She says she wakes up easily. There's not a lot of distance between houses here. I bet a silencer was used."

"See to it someone interviews the occupants of the other three houses later on today."

"I'll see to it."

"Keep up the good work, and maybe you'll be sheriff one day."

"A pay raise would suffice."

"Second that."

"Was the bed slept in?"

"Yes, but a lot of single men don't bother to make their beds up every day, so can't be sure."

"Any medicines in the bathroom?"

"Just low-dose aspirin. The bathroom is messy but nothing out of the ordinary, what with no wife to pick up after the guy."

"No wife—how do you know that?"

"Well, no women's clothes anywhere, so unless she runs around naked all the time, no wife."

"Your logic is impeccable."

CHAPTER FORTY-TWO

Buddy had informed the victim's parents of their son's death that evening. If there were any lieutenant chores he despised more than death announcements, he couldn't name them.

Mr. Post had taken it well, asking questions to which Buddy couldn't yet answer. He agreed to put off the interviews till the next morning. He knew of no enemies or death threats to his son.

The next morning Sergeant Bobby Rizzo met with the Posts at their home.

"I'm very sorry to impose on you in your time of grief, but the likelihood of this being a murder forces us to call on you."

"We understand."

"Vic was single?"

"Yes. He never married."

"Does he have any siblings?"

"One brother who lives in Tallahassee. We called him last evening, and he should be here in an hour or so."

"Did they get along?" Bobby's eyes bored into the father's eyes.

"They were never close, but they didn't have any conflicts."

"Is he married?"

Mr. Post was hesitant. "Not exactly. He's gay and has had a companion, as he calls him, for four years."

"You've met him?"

"Oh, yes. Seems like a nice person."

"I have to ask you how your will is structured."

Mr. Post was shocked! "My wife receives the benefits from the whole estate. When she passes, the estate is divided equally between the two sons. I can't imagine—"

"I know. As I said, I'm forced to ask these questions."

"He had been going to Las Vegas some of late. I was afraid he'd been gambling."

"When did you last know he'd been there?"

"Maybe a month ago or so. I hear they don't like debtors out there."

"They can't collect a debt from a dead person. Not likely them."

"How about that girl that seduced those four boys back in high school?"

"She's saved the lives of two of them recently. You didn't hear?"

"No."

Bobby gave them a synopsis of the two events.

"So you see, she showed forgiveness, and by the way, it wasn't seduction. It was rape." There was a hint of anger in Bobby.

"Could you call your other son's cell phone and find out when he will be getting here?"

Mr. Post could and he did. "Ten minutes. You're welcome to wait for him here if you wish."

"That would be helpful. This is a coroner's case, you understand. He's been sent to the morgue, and a postmortem will be done this morning."

"We understand."

"Your son was significantly overweight. Was he always that way?"

"No. Just in the last year or two. I had talked to him about it, but he just laughed it off."

"Did he enjoy his teaching?"

"Very much so. We never heard him speak of a downside to it."

"I'm also going to meet with his students briefly to see if they have anything to offer."

"Really?"

"We try to touch all the bases."

"Would you care for a cup of coffee?"

"Thank you. That would be nice."

"It's that single-cup type. Really good."

Bobby wasn't even through with his coffee when Sterling Post pulled in to the driveway.

Chapter Forty-Three

Introductions were made.

"We haven't received the final postmortem report, but it appears someone did a clumsy job of faking a suicide," Bobby said.

Sterling was as thin as his brother was fat. He was immaculately but not overly dressed.

He had a gold Rolex on his left hand and a gold necklace around his neck. He seemed to glide across the floor and had a becoming smile.

"Happy to meet you, sir. Very sorry about the circumstances."

Bobby expected a limp handshake but received a surprisingly firm one instead. "Have you any idea who might have done this?"

"Well, his gambling friends might have been despondent over his debts."

"He told you of them?"

"Yes, and he tried to borrow money from me."

"You never told us that!" his father said.

"I've tried not to burden you with bad things all my life."

"Your father brought up the gambling too. You can't get a debt payment from a dead person."

"You could set an example for others, couldn't you?"

"There is that. Your brother was shot around nine o'clock. Can you tell me where you and your companion were at that time?"

Mrs. Post was shocked!

"In our apartment, with two others, playing bridge. Knowing you would be asking that question, I have their names and phone numbers here."

Sterling handed Bobby a piece of paper.

CHAPTER FORTY-FOUR

Bobby Rizzo obtained permission to communicate with the class that the late Victor Post had taught.

"My name is Bobby Rizzo. I'm a homicide detective here in town. I'm investigating the murder of your teacher. I'm here to see what, if anything, any of you can tell me about your late teacher. Firstly, was he right- or left-handed?"

There was a momentary silence.

"Left. No doubt about it," a boy said. Most of the other students nodded in agreement.

"We thought so. His murder was crudely staged so as to resemble a suicide. They used his right hand to hold the gun after he was shot. People doing this themselves always use their dominant hand. You've helped us already. We thought he was left-handed and now you've confirmed it. Thank you."

"Now he had gained a lot of weight in the past year. Do any of you know how or why this happened?"

The same boy said, "In the cafeteria, he usually ate twice as much as most of us did. Second helpings all over the place." More affirmative head-nodding.

"Any idea why he did that?"

"We thought he had a crush on another one of the teachers here, and she didn't reciprocate."

Giggles came from the students.

"Anything else?"

"We really liked the guy, and he liked us. We all chipped in to buy a big flower arrangement for his funeral."

"Wow! You guys are something else! Good for you! Was he ever unfair or unkind to any of you?"

The answer came almost unanimously. "No!"

"Did he have any problems with anybody here at school?"

The class members looked more to be reticent than negational.

"Your principal gave me permission to dismiss your class when I'm done here. Thank you for your cooperation and attention. I'll stay here for a few minutes longer in case any of you want to tell me something in private."

The only student who stayed with Bobby was the young man who had been the most vocal before.

"I do appreciate your help."

"You're welcome. We really liked the guy and hope you find his killer."

"Something you want to tell me?"

Looking around to be sure nobody else was lurking nearby, the student said, "He was gay."

Bobby wasn't scandalized. "Did he make a move on any of the students?"

"Not that we knew of—and we'd know if he had."

"How about any of the other teachers?"

"The science teacher. Didn't last long. I think he started his binge eating after that."

"How do you know about that?"

The boy gave a small smile. "The whole class knew about it. We're cool with it. Most of our parents aren't."

"But nothing with any of the students?"

"No, sir."

"Anything else?"

"Yes. You any relation to the Cubs' first-base man?"

"Not that I know of. You kids are so much savvier than my group was."

"Electronic devices. Good and bad news travel fast."

Chapter Forty-Five

With a little help from the principal, Bobby was able to derive four staff members' names to interview relative to Victor Post's murder. Two uninvolved names were added to insulate the two members he really wanted to interview.

"Thanks for seeing me, Ms. Swanson. I'm trying to collect all the information I can to better understand Mr. Post."

"Happy to cooperate, but I know very little about him that's not common knowledge."

"I've been told that he had a crush on you. Did he?"

"Yes, but nothing ever came of it."

"Why not?"

"In case nobody else has told you, he was gay. He just wanted a good friend, and I was already as friendly with him as I cared to be."

"Did he ever talk to you about his gambling?"

"Not much. He said it was a bad habit."

"His weight gain started about the time you didn't become his good friend. Was that the case?"

"I guess so. I never thought about it."

"Did he ever talk to you about his family, his brother in particular?"

"Said he was gay too. Seemed it ran in the family."

"Is there anybody around here who actively disliked him?"

Ms. Swanson paused. "No, not really. Are you seeing Dave Hudman here?"

Bobby checked his notes. "Matter of fact, I am."

"I believe Victor offered to be his best friend."

"What came of that?"

"Nothing, as far as I know."

"Was either of them angry about things?"

"Not that I know of."

"His students seemed to be very fond of him. They pitched in and bought a big bouquet of flowers in his name and sent them to the funeral home."

"Wonder what they'd do for me."

Bobby smiled. "I understand your students are very fond of you too."

"They are?"

"That's what I heard."

Bobby was in the habit of boosting morale, even when it might not be deserved.

CHAPTER FORTY-SIX

"Thanks for seeing me, Mr. Hudman."

"I'm a big supporter of the men in blue. Happy to."

"What can you tell me about Mr. Post?"

"I don't know anybody who actively disliked him. He had a crush on one of the ladies here, I heard."

"That didn't work out, did it?"

"Well, no. They were of differing persuasions."

"He liked you a lot."

"Well, I liked him but not in the way he wanted to be liked."

"You knew of his gambling?"

"Yes. Everybody did."

"Was it in response to his business with Ms. Swanson?"

"About then, I guess."

"And his overeating?"

"Probably."

"What else can you tell me about him?"

"He confided to me that he had participated in a gang rape in high school and hadn't been able to get with a woman since. He told me more about himself than I wanted to know."

"Did he talk much about his family?"

"No. He has a brother. He's gay too, he told me."

"No abuse?"

"I guess not."

"His murder was crudely staged to appear to be a suicide."

"I didn't do it, and I don't have the foggiest notion who did."

"We don't either, but we will. Thanks again for your cooperation."

Bobby did pro forma interviews with the other two teachers.

They were of no help to him, but he had a positive effect on them. They would tell anyone who would listen about their police interviews.

Chapter Forty-Seven

Buddy Short had tried and tried to figure out who benefited from Victor Post's murder.

His only sibling, Sterling, would double his inheritance, whenever that came to pass, but he had three witnesses who swore they were playing bridge with him in Tallahassee at the time of the murder.

His debt to gamblers would be forfeit if they had killed him. If May's father had sought to kill him, it should have happened six years ago.

Nothing at the school where he taught rose to a motive level. The students loved him. There was no hint of any molestation behavior. Ramifications of his sexual orientation seemed benign, from what he had been told.

The murder weapon had the identification numbers completely filed off and could not be traced back to anybody, including himself.

There was no evidence of any forced entry to Victor's apartment. His phone records and credit card usage pointed nowhere at all.

Could he have killed himself, purposely faking an easy-to-be-deduced murder? Remotely possible. Makes no sense—but then lots of murders made no sense to uninvolved persons.

His two surviving classmates that were complicit and participated in his assault on May Stover had no identifiable contact with him on the phone records available.

May's having saved the lives of the other two should make her majorly unlikely as the culprit.

So "nobody" did it, but Victor was still murdered.

As the king of Siam said, "Is a puzzlement."

CHAPTER FORTY-EIGHT

Dr. Prince visited May periodically to see how her newly discovered powers were progressing.

On one of his visits, he confided to her that barring the unexpected, she should live to be two hundred years old.

"How do you know that?"

"I just do. My wife and I are the same age, but I look many years younger. She knows of this enhanced life expectancy and is accepting of the implications. My son has my—and your—traits. My daughter does not." That would take some getting used to!

One of the busybodied nurses said to another nurse not so afflicted, "You think they're having an affair?"

"Probably one of those afternoon quickies, wouldn't you guess?"

Offended, the busybodied one flounced off.

May wondered how to broach the subject to Matt. It could be a big turnoff for him. He likely wouldn't believe her and would think she was delusional. Another turnoff. She loved him, and she decided not to bring it up at all—for now.

She had a vision, one day, that the backup hospital generators were faulty. Stupid vision!

Nonetheless she called the engineer and told him about it.

"How do you know this?"

"I just do. Please check it out."

Crazy female! He checked the system out anyway and found it was indeed screwed up! By calling in help, he was able to get the system operational by dark.

At 2:00 AM the biggest lightning storm in years knocked out transformers all over the city, including the hospital's.

There are almost always patients on electrically run devices that are life-sustaining. Such was the case that night. The hospital lost power. The backups kicked in without a hitch. No problem. Six hours later, the electricity came back on, and the generators turned off.

The engineer was thoroughly perplexed. How could the nurse possibly have known about the defect? He decided to say nothing to anyone till he talked to her. Problem was, he didn't know who she was.

He saved the handwritten note to him from the hospital's administrator, praising him for having all things in order when the blackout occurred.

CHAPTER FORTY-NINE

Matt Heller had the honor of being the top Ford salesman in the southeast in the third quarter. Literally translated, it meant he had sold the most cars. His success was based in no small measure on his being able to communicate with people of all ages. He could register approval of a nose ring in a young rebel and the hearing aid of an older person. Good humor but not farcical. Honest.

Being on commission, there was no cash to go with his "attaboy" pronouncement. He did get a favorable picture on a billboard.

His cohorts envied his achievements but also admired his common touch. Several of them tried to emulate his approach, meeting with limited success.

May was ever so proud of him. They were heading toward marriage, and she had not told him of the depth of her prescience.

They were having dinner at Seasons 52. He'd sold three more cars that day.

"Do you think the billboard picture does me justice?"

"I don't think any picture can really do that."

"I thought that. Do you think I should start giving out autographs?"

"Only if you charge for them."

Sometimes they would have a glass of wine before their dinner. Sometimes not. This was a not time. She needed to tell him about her gift.

"Matt, I need to talk to you about something."

"You're actually a Martian?"

"You're maybe close. You know how I sometimes can anticipate things that do come to pass? Often, they are merely informational, but sometimes they are important. These visions come to me unsolicited. I can't summon them up."

"You're entirely serious, aren't you?"

"Yes, I am. I had one last evening that involves you."

That got his attention!

"There will be a customer you will see tomorrow afternoon who is using an alias. He plans to steal the car he test-drives with you. He will ask you to drive the return leg so he can make an important phone call. He will get out of the car, and when you are out of the car and at the back of it, he will jump in the car and take off. He's not dangerous, so you can turn off the engine while you are exchanging places and thwart his plan. You could also tell him you are warning all the other car agencies about his plan and that he should consider getting a real job. I would still have my gun with me in case he gets rambunctious."

"That's all?"

"Pretty much."

They had the most excellent meal they had expected, and afterward, Matt took her back to her apartment.

"Want to come in for a few hours?"

He did.

"You didn't anticipate this, did you?"

"Want to bet?"

May went to sleep easily after their activities. Matt was all hyped up about his upcoming adventure and found Morpheus's arms elusive.

CHAPTER FIFTY

Don Barney finally had his jaws emancipated from their wired restraints. Chewing his first food in six weeks was not painful at all. That was a pleasant surprise. His jaw did tire out easily, however.

He had lost close to fifteen pounds, despite all the protein drinks he had downed. He had no doubt he would find those lost pounds in short order.

He thought that he hadn't really thanked May enough for saving his life. How can you do justice to that anyway? He'd try.

The medical school had cut him some slack because of his injuries. He did not fall behind. He was a good student, even when wounded. Much study in med school is predicated on foregoing study, so failing to keep up with the work could and did cause dropouts.

He had May's address, so he started with a nice bouquet of flowers. May, without looking at the enclosed card, immediately called Matt to thank him.

"Uh, I didn't send any flowers," Matt said.

May pulled out the card and saw Don's name.

"They're from that guy with the broken jaw. Sorry for my mistake. No visions on his one."

Matt was just the least bit jealous. "I'm not sure how you show appreciation for someone saving your life."

"It just has a brief note thanking me."

"Do I need to send you an even bigger bouquet to keep up?"

"You're not only leading the race, there are no other contestants."

That got Matt unjealous.

Chapter Fifty-One

Luigi recognized that he was at least infatuated with Pam. What to do—or at least try to do?

If he could get her to go to New York with him, would she be turned off by the way he made his living? Would his father accept her? He decided to do what was best for her. Major problem—how could he determine that?

Pam was similarly at loose ends. She had deep feelings for Luigi, and she had no major ties to Florida. What would likely happen if she went to New York with him? Would his father disapprove of her because she wasn't Italian? It was apparent that the family was in to the rackets. She didn't have disdain for the people who sold drugs. Nobody forced anybody to use them. It was entirely optional. It was dangerous, of course, all the way around. She was totally against murder, and she suspected that Luigi was sent to Jacksonville to avenge the death of his brother if he thought it were indicated. Her testimony had derailed that option.

She could have a trial stay with him. If it didn't work out, she could always return to Jacksonville or go somewhere new. She needed to have a frank talk with him and make a decision.

"I'm overdue in my return to New York. I must go tomorrow. I want you to go with me, but I want what's best for you even more," Luigi said to Pam.

"What do you think of a trial visit? No commitment. If it doesn't work out for us, it could be 'It was great fun, but it was just one of those things.'"

They sealed it with a kiss—for starters.

CHAPTER FIFTY-TWO

Luigi (Lou) was able to get Pam a seat on the flight to New York City. She hastily packed the night before. He assured her there would be places in New York to obtain whatever she might have overlooked.

The flight to LaGuardia was uneventful. Pam had never been to New York City, so this was exciting in and of itself.

Luigi had scheduled a limo to take them to his home. It didn't exactly whisk them there, but it did get them there. He and his father had separate suites in the mansion. A maid helped them with their luggage and had water, wine, and some little sandwiches placed in their capacious room.

"Did this used to be a bowling alley?"

"Not that I know of, but there is a swimming pool out back."

It was time for Pam to ask. "Just what do you do?"

"We cater to the baser instincts of a significant segment of humanity. Drugs and women. No children involved, and the girls are all consensual. Shocked?"

"Not in the least. Your mother living?"

"She passed a couple of years ago. Lung cancer. She smoked up till two days before she died."

"But you don't."

"Never. Filthy habit. So you're okay with things so far?"

"I am, but there's your father to meet."

"I predict he will love you. Be just yourself, and that will happen."

Dinner was served!

"Dad, this is Pam Spicer," Luigi said, introducing his companion.

"Pleased to meet you, Ms. Spicer. I believe you have cast a spell over my son."

"Or he over me," Pam replied.

Luigi's father gave a big laugh. "You do like lobster, don't you?"

"Yes, what few times I've had it."

"My son tells me you do not have a job because you don't need one."

"I'm an orphan and comfortable. I do know how to work, however."

"You were friends with our Guido?"

"Just friends. He made the mistake of protecting me where I didn't need it."

CHAPTER FIFTY-THREE

Pam didn't put on airs. She just projected herself as she really was. She liked Lou's father, and she felt he liked her.

The family actually did own an import business, and it had been successful. After a couple of days of doing mostly nothing and awaiting Lou's return, Pam decided she needed to find something to occupy her time.

At dinner on her third evening in New York, she brought the subject up.

"I've worked retail sales in a number of places. How about giving me a chance in your store?"

That surprised both Lou and his father.

"We can try it on and see if it fits," Lou's father said.

"Thank you. May I see the store tomorrow?"

"Of course. My manager is efficient and affable. You should get along well with her. Lou, will you see to it tomorrow?"

"Sure."

"Something I want to tell you both is that I have prostate cancer. It is slow growing, and my doctor says I'm more likely to die with it than from it. He suggests that I slow down a bit, more from my age than the cancer. That means if Lou plans to succeed me in our business, he'll need to be getting more involved."

"I will do whatever is required," Lou replied.

"And I'll see that he does," Pam said.

"How do you like the codfish?"

"Love it. You may notice, I ate every bite of it."

"Would you care for more?"

"If I wanted to get fat. Thanks, no."

"I'm off to bed. Thank you for straightening my son out."

"I didn't know I was crooked," Lou said.

CHAPTER FIFTY-FOUR

Matt wasn't worried, but he was hyped up over the prospect of May's prediction that he would have a customer the next day who would try to steal a new car he was "test-driving."

The salesmen at the automobile pavilion were on a rotational basis when it came to visitors.

Matt had already sold one car before 10:00 AM. His next turn didn't come till just before noon.

He shook the man's hand and greeted him. He told Matt his name was Joe Jones and he was interested in a Ford Taurus, preferably an off-white one.

"Good choice. There are a lot of them around, and unless you want some funky colored one, we can fill your bill. Would this be financed with us or elsewhere?"

"Cash." (Always a delight to a salesman.)

"What line of work are you in?"

The buyer was hesitant. "I'm a plumber."

"And a very frugal one at that." Matt was all smiles.

"I work hard and don't buy what I can't afford."

Matt had noticed the man's hands when he shook one—perfectly manicured and cared for, not a single callous to be seen. *He's the one!* he thought.

"Joe Jones is your name, you said?"

"Right, pretty common."

As they walked to the car lot, Matt told him all about the safety features such as front-end collision avoidance, blind side dots on the mirrors, rearview camera, and keyless ignition.

"Well, here's the little beauty."

"The paper here lists it at forty-two-thousand dollars. Can you do any better than that?"

Matt decided to continue to play the game, in case the guy was legit.

"Other dealerships jack up their alleged prices so they can give you a big fake discount. We don't do it that way. Our printed prices are authentic. Are you ex-military?"

"Yes. I am."

"Well, you're in luck. If you buy a car within the current week, you'll get a thousand-dollar check back from Ford."

"Really? Can we test-drive it?"

"We sure can."

Matt procured the key fob and handed it to the man. "They make me verify that you have a driver's license."

"No problem."

To Matt it looked legitimate—it still might be.

Matt had him drive to a street that was lightly traveled.

"How do you like it?"

"I love it. Can you drive it back? I've got an important phone call to make."

This is it! Matt thought.

They both exited the car. As Joe Jones (or whomever he really was) walked to the back of the car, Matt walked to the front, but not before turning the engine off.

The man jumped into the car and locked the doors. He smiled benignly at Matt and pressed the ignition button. Nothing happened.

"Oh, I forgot to tell you. The key fob has to be inside the car to work."

Fright! Panic! Anxiety!

"Look, let's go back to the dealership and talk about this," Joe said.

"There's nothing to talk about, Joe. Get out of the car now, and don't try to pull a gun on me. I have one too."

Joe got out of the car with a severe case of the trembles.

"Go stand on the curb over there."

He did.

"I'm going back to the dealership and telling my boss what you tried to pull. Whether the cops are involved or not will be up to him. I have your fingerprints here on the steering wheel, which might interest the police, and I'm going to alert the other car dealerships in the area about you."

"You leaving me here?"

"I am. Try getting a real job and have a nice day."

CHAPTER FIFTY-FIVE

Matt's boss was all ears when he heard the tale of the attempted hijacking of the car.

"What tipped you off?"

Matt wasn't about to mention May.

"He said he was a plumber, but his hands were well manicured. Didn't compute."

"You been reading Sherlock Holmes lately? That's amazing!"

"So what are you going to do about it?"

"It's your call. You earned it."

Matt paused. "No harm was done. I do want to alert our fellow dealerships about it."

"Good PR too," his manager said. "Would you have any interest in being assistant manager here?"

"Would I make as much money as I do in sales?"

"I guess not. Well done, Matt."

Matt knew May would be on tenterhooks about the incident, so he called her on her cell phone and just told her it had happened just as she'd said and he'd tell her the whole story that evening.

Matt had a casual lunch. There was plenty of time to ruminate about the adventure. Then he went back to work. It was his turn to entertain the visitor.

"How do you do, sir? I'm Matt Heller. What can we do for you today?"

"I'm interested in the new Taurus. I hear they're going to quit making them next year."

"That's what we've heard also. Any particular color?"

"Do you have one that's really off the wall?"

One car that had come to the dealership by mistake was a garish green.

It had been collecting dust in their lot for three months. Not one person had shown any interest in it. Matt had coined the name of the color as Urp Green.

"We do. One really leaps to mind. That's it over there. Misty Green is the color.

"I love it!" There was dust on the invoice attached to the window, but it was legible.

"Forty-two thousand. Is that your best price?"

"We may be able to do a bit better. Are you a veteran?"

"Matter of fact, I am. Navy—twenty-six years."

"Well, you're in luck! If you buy a new Ford this week, the company will send you a check for a thousand dollars. How about that?"

"Is that so? That's a real incentive. May I test-drive it?"

"Of course."

Matt got the key fob and handed it to the gentleman.

"Lordy! I completely forgot to ask your name."

"Bill Jones."

"You don't have a brother named Joe, do you?"

He didn't.

Chapter Fifty-Six

As Matt was picking May up for a dinner out, she was as anxious to hear of his adventure as he was to present it.

"So you told him to have a nice day and drove off?"

"Yep. When he thought he had control of the car, with me on the outside, he had a snarky smile on his face. I loved it when he first realized he couldn't start the car and he went from snarky to crestfallen. So sad."

"And his nails tipped you off?"

"Sure did. No self-respecting plumber would be going around without a callous here and there."

"And you didn't tell anyone I had tipped you off?"

"No. I didn't think you wanted to come all the way out right yet."

"That's right. I'm so happy for you. You're a hero."

"My manager left it to me as to what to do about it. We informed all the other car dealerships in the county about the scam. We didn't bother with the police. No harm, no foul with them. Oh, and he offered me the assistant managership."

"Wonderful!"

"Not exactly. It pays less than I make selling cars."

"All you do is wonderful, that aside!"

"And you're the power behind the throne, you know."

"All right, knave. When doth thou marry the fair maid?"

"Three months? That'll give your parents time to participate."

"Done! Your place or mine tonight?"

"We're here, and it's dark outside. I vote here."

"It's not dark enough inside."

She rectified that.

CHAPTER FIFTY-SEVEN

May's parents were middle-of-the-road people. Upper middle class. Helen Stover had done secretarial work till her two daughters were born and had returned to that sort of job after the girls matured. Her husband, George, was the manager of a Home Depot store, having worked his way up from stock boy. They were solid citizens.

May's older sister had considered a nursing career, but an early marriage and pregnancy made her a housewife instead. Their little family lived within their means and were happy in Orlando. Her husband, George, was an artist, employed by Disney. His job description was hard to define.

Their two offspring were normal healthy children that didn't see their grandparents as often as the grandparents thought they should. May's relationship with her sister was casual.

May awakened abruptly one morning, having had a disturbing dream and/or vision. It had to do with a little Chinese restaurant her parents liked. Matt had roused up and sensed something was amiss.

"Something wrong?"

"Oh, I remember you. We're getting married or something, aren't we?"

Matt answered, looking perplexed, "Yes, yes, I believe we are. Such being the case, how about a kiss?"

She still had a worried look as they kissed.

"Okay, what is it?" Matt asked.

"My folks like this Chinese restaurant, and I had a dream that something very bad will happen there tomorrow."

"Like what?"

"I don't know, but I've got to warn them."

"So call them right now."

"Hi, Mom—" May began as her mother answered the phone.

"What's wrong?"

"Nothing with me. Do you still go to the Snappy Dragon restaurant?"

"Yes. In fact, I'm going there tomorrow. They have these take-out fully prepared meals that all you do is heat them."

"I had a disturbing dream last night. Something very bad will happen there tomorrow."

"Only a dream?"

May was intense! "Please, humor me. Go there today or two days from now!"

"You sound agitated. You sure you're all right?"

Chapter Fifty-Eight

May got up early the following morning so she could catch the morning news before going to work. Fifteen minutes and not a word about the Chinese restaurant or much about anything anywhere that was bad. *It will show up this evening,* she thought.

Evening news—nothing.

Her mother had kept her word and had gone to the restaurant the day before the anticipated untoward event. She, too, had sought the news. Nothing. Evening—more nothing.

"I told you nothing would come of it," her husband said.

"You've had the same food last night you would have gotten had I gone yesterday. Besides, I promised her I wouldn't go. You do still honor promises, don't you?"

The next evening Matt came to pick May up.

"Nothing. Can we watch the news before we go out?" May said.

"Of course. Just because you were spot on with my attempted car theft doesn't mean you have to be entirely accurate every time. Besides, she could just as well go there one day or the other. No harm done."

"Right or wrong, you back me, don't you?"

"Absotively!"

Matt could tell during dinner that May was distracted. That would pass.

She wasn't distracted enough that she didn't respond to his goodnight kisses etc. Especially the *etc.*

Chapter Fifty-Nine

It took almost a week for the news to break.

Salmonella outbreak. One person had died, a second one was in a coma, and twelve other people had been sickened. The offending agent was said to be romaine lettuce served in the Snappy Dragon Chinese restaurant.

It seemed the restaurant had acquired this lettuce from an unlicensed source, which had been summarily shut down, as had the restaurant.

May didn't have to scan the back pages. This was front-page news! She just might have saved both her parents' lives. She could only speak briefly to her mother, whom she awakened.

"Read the paper, Mom?"

"Just got up. What's up?"

"Your Chinese restaurant is closed because of a salmonella-poisoned batch of romaine. You weren't buying any that day you didn't go there?"

"My God! You saved us both from the stuff!"

"One person is dead and another in coma, so you may have been saved from something worse. Love you. Gotta run."

"Oh, George, that was May," Mary said to her husband as soon as she hung up.

"What did she have? Another one of her visions?" George smirked.

"Why, no, dear. Here's the morning paper. Enjoy it."

He wondered why she was acting so happy till he saw the headline.

He then knew what he would be eating that night—crow!

CHAPTER SIXTY

Buddy Short and Bobby Rizzo were commiserating together over the disappointment with certain cases they had been working on. A few were nearing the dreaded "cold" status. One in particular was the murder of a teacher where the perpetrator had done a poor job of faking a suicide. The victim had flaws such as gambling and obesity. He had been gay, so that presented other factors. All the known principals had alibis that seemed valid. No hostility seemed to present itself.

"The brother was said to be playing bridge in Gainesville at the time of the shooting. We have affidavits from the other three players attesting to the time. The brothers weren't close, but there was no evidence of any discord between them. Nothing at school. No 'companions' to judge. Help me, Bobby!"

"I wish I could. His parents both have conditions that should shorten their lives. They're comfortable but not rich. I guess the brother could wish to double his potential inheritance. Maybe we should rule out perjury among the three bridge partners."

"Our buddies over there got corroboration of sorts. Nobody could say they weren't there as advertised."

"I could go over there and rattle some chains."

"I don't have any better ideas. Go for it."

Bobby knew Gainesville pretty well. He'd gotten his degree there in criminology. He went to one of his former teachers and spoke to him between classes.

"Bobby Rizzo! You were one of my best students. You're in Jacksonville, aren't you?"

"Yes, sir. We have a case over there that is close to the cold hopper. The murder victim's brother is in school over here and was allegedly playing bridge at the time of the murder."

"I presume the other three vouched for him?"

"They did. There is some inheritance in the mix, and the victim was his only sibling. We never underestimate the love of money."

"The Bible says that the love of money is the source of all evil. I believe that. Are you going to talk to them?"

"Yes. They all four live in the same dorm."

"I believe you have a couple of little ones, don't you?"

"I do."

"I have a couple of big ones I'm proud of. Well, happy hunting."

CHAPTER SIXTY-ONE

Bobby had contacted the late Victor Post's brother, Sterling, to set up a time when he could interview the bridge foursome who had presented his alibi for the time of his brother's shooting.

The four of them had spacious apartments in a development that catered to students. Sterling had assembled the other three in his own.

Once they were all seated, Sterling said, "We told the local officers that we were playing bridge at the time of my brother's shooting."

Bobby decided to state something fictional. "We have found testimony to the contrary. If by chance Mr. Post here is found to have done the shooting, all three of you will be held guilty as accessories to murder. That could get all of you ten years in prison. Anyone have a comment?"

"Mr. Rizzo, I did not shoot anyone, and I was here at the time of the shooting," Sterling said.

"Anyone else have anything to say?"

The physically smallest of the four blurted out, "This has gone far enough! We four were in town, but we weren't playing bridge!"

"Shut up, Silas!"

"No, you shut the hell up! I'm not doing ten years in prison for anyone!"

"Let Silas speak!" Bobby said threateningly.

"We were at a local whorehouse at the time. I used a credit card there you can check out, and Sterling used one too."

"So how about it, Sterling?"

"Okay, okay. That's where we were. I did use my credit card there. Gainesville Social Club."

"Why didn't you say so in the first place and save us all a lot of trouble?"

"It's nothing to brag about. I'm sorry. It seemed right at the time."

"I was told you were gay, Sterling. Was I misinformed?"

"Massively. The advantages of pretending include getting girls to feel at ease with you, and then there are those that want to change your 'persuasion' and feel triumphant when they do."

"I'll be damned. Do you remember the lady's name?"

"Penelope—she's the only Penelope there."

Sterling wrote down the brothel's address. "Be sure to tell them I sent you—there'd be a finder's fee available for me."

CHAPTER SIXTY-TWO

"Well, hello there, handsome, what can we do for you?"

"Firstly, I don't care what you do or don't do here. I'm from Jacksonville, and I am investigating a murder there."

"Like you're a cop?"

"Very like. All I want is information about one of your contestants on this night."

Bobby handed her a piece of paper.

"Oh, that cat! Dressed like hyper gay. Penny looked after him and said he was a real stallion."

"I need only two minutes of her time."

"Luckily, she's twixt and tween—I'll get her."

Although she had been reassured as to Rizzo's needs, the girl in question appeared to be very anxious.

"Penelope, is it?"

"Yeah, but everybody calls me Penny."

Bobby showed her a picture of Sterling.

"On yeah! Some dude. Dressed like he's part girl. Like to wore me out!"

"Did he say anything about anything?"

"We didn't do much talking, as I recall."

"Were there other men with him?"

"Three others, I heard. Never saw 'em."

"Thanks for your time, Penny."

"Sure you wouldn't care for a little nap before you go back to Jacksonville?"

Bobby laughed. "No, but if I do need one sometime, I'll look you up."

Bobby didn't laugh much on the way home.

"Four-and-a-half percent unemployment, and she ends up there. Damn it!"

Chapter Sixty-Three

Early the next morning, Bobby reported to Buddy about the illumination of his Gainesville trip.

"Well, have you come up with the killer?"

"No, but I've pretty well ruled one out."

"How is that?"

"The foursome was not been playing bridge as had been reported."

"So?"

"First I want to tell you about my stopover at the brothel."

"As in 'house of ill fame'?"

"That's the one. I have established a working relationship with Penelope there."

"Your work or hers?"

"That will become manifest. The bridge foursome was at the pleasure place rather than at the bridge table at the time of Mr. Post's demise. Research there and credit card corroboration validated that. Sterling is not our man."

"I was rather hoping you would come up with who is rather than who isn't."

"Me too, but it wasn't to be."

"How much of this are you going to tell your wife about?"

"Precious little."

"Good judgment."

CHAPTER SIXTY-FOUR

Pam's salesperson job in the Silentia Import enterprise went well. The manager there was a motherly sort who took a shine to Pam. Being Luigi's girlfriend was a good credential too.

Pointing to a large concrete elephant statue, Pam asked, "Do people really buy this sort of thing?"

"Oh yes. There is a group of people in our economic upper class who constantly try to outdo each other in a lot of things, including lawn decorations. I'll bet this sells within three days."

"You a betting woman?" Pam asked.

"Sometimes."

"I'll bet you a whole dollar that the elephant will still be here a week from today."

"I usually hate to take advantage of my employees, but it's sometimes necessary to put them in their place. So you're on."

They shook hands and went about their business, which, at the moment, included four separate shoppers.

"May I help you, ma'am?"

"I hope so. Our outdoor decorations are so unimaginative and passé. Do you have some items that are one of a kind?"

"Matter of fact, we do. Take a look at this pristine, special concrete elephant, which just arrived from Africa."

"Inside or outside?"

"Either. To be fair, when I said this was one of a kind, I mean in so far as we know. I certainly have never seen the likes of it."

"How heavy is it?"

"It's on the tag here, I believe."

"Two hundred-twenty pounds it says."

"The heavier the better!"

"Well, I'd guess you would need a live one to be any heavier."

"What is your price?"

"I'll have to ask my manager. It just came in, so we haven't tagged it yet."

"Mrs. Tuggle, this nice lady wants to know the price for this artistic elephant."

"Hello, Mrs. Styvacent. How have been?"

"A few little nuisances here and there. Nothing major bad. They did screw up our reservations for the presidential suite on the Bostonian ship. Left us with one of those executive suites, if you can imagine such a thing."

"I hope you plan vengeance by exploiting the free beverage package."

"We've already made plans for that."

"I'm almost embarrassed to tell you the price. It's three thousand dollars."

"When can you have it delivered?"

"Is this afternoon soon enough?"

"Yes. You just spoil me every time I'm in here."

She made the check out and handed it to Pam.

"You give this sweet girl a nice commission!"

"I certainly will," Mrs. Tuggle said aloud. "Less one dollar," she said under her breath.

Chapter Sixty-Five

By the next time May visited her parents, the salmonella story was old news. The comatose patient had died. The Chinese restaurant was to be closed indefinitely.

Attorneys were circling the field, salivating over the liability prospects.

"We plan to get married three months from now. We want a small wedding. You certainly can ask anybody you wish but with a minimum of people that don't even know me. Matt has told his family his same wishes."

"Where would you like the ceremony performed?" her mother asked.

"How about your church?"

"I'd like that very much. They can do a catered reception there too, if you wished. They can handle up to a hundred people easily."

May glanced at Matt. "Sounds good to me."

"No more than twenty-five at a rehearsal dinner—wherever."

"May I use your old wedding dress?"

Mary Stover was stunned! Tears! "Of course."

"How's work?" May's father asked.

"Going well. They can't make cars fast enough to keep up with Matt's volume."

"About that salmonella business, I didn't believe that there was a problem. I don't understand how you could possibly have known in advance about it," her father said.

"I didn't know what the nature of the danger would be. I only was convinced there was a reason to keep you from going to the restaurant."

"Do you have these visions often?"

"They come unannounced. I can't summon them."

"She has a special gift that defies explanation. Here's what she anticipated for me." Matt went on with the whole story about the attempted hijacking of the car.

"I recall her as a child one time when we were at a ballgame together. She said, 'Watch out for the ball!' There was a foul ball blasted our way five seconds after she said that."

Back to the wedding plans. May picked her sister to be the maid of honor, and Matt chose his father to be his best man.

"The wedding dress may need a little taking in here and there," May's mother said.

They said their goodbyes and departed.

"I don't think we should tell our friends about May's unusual ability."

"Heavens no!"

CHAPTER SIXTY-SIX

Bobby thought he had cleaned up the waters in Gainesville only to have them muddied anew. Sterling Post did not shoot his brother.

He was well acquainted with the love of money being the source of all evil. Sterling's parents were chronically ill, with limited life expectancies, and they were not rich but well-off.

Bobby researched the family structure of the Posts. The mother had one sister two years younger than herself. She was a widow with one son who was attending junior college in Jacksonville. Sterling's father had been an orphan and had no known relatives. The widow and son were said to be at their home at the time of the shooting of Victor Post. No neighbor of theirs could say otherwise.

In the middle of his ruminations, Bobby received a call from his friend and counterpart in Gainesville.

"Hey, Bobby. That Sterling Post guy you came over to see last week was shot and is touch and go for survival."

"Any leads?"

"Not really. Who gets the money if he joins his brother?"

"You mean their parents' money?"

"Anybody's."

"The parents are chronically ill. The father has no relatives whatsoever. The mother has one sister here in Jacksonville. She's a widow with a twenty-year-old son. He's in junior college here. They said they were home at the time of Victor's shooting, and none of the neighbors could say otherwise. Looks like the sister gets promoted to next of kin if Sterling doesn't make it."

"Lots of smoke. I'll keep you posted about Sterling. Family okay— yours, I mean?"

"Yes. Yours?"

"Mean as ever. Love her unconditionally."

"That's a pretty big word for a country cop."

"Hey, we all have running water and electricity over here."

"Are the Indians pacified?"

"If we keep them away from firewater."

"Are we being politically incorrect?"

"You don't tell, I don't tell."

CHAPTER SIXTY-SEVEN

Luigi and Pat were having dinner at a nice upscale restaurant not far from Luigi's home. Pat had noticed that Lew was never focused on his dinners. He was always scanning his surroundings. It made her a little uncomfortable.

He stopped in midsentence and whispered to her, "Go to the lady's' room right now—please!"

She got up immediately, glancing at the front door of the restaurant where two burly men had just entered. They were ignoring the receptionist and scanning the room. She could do nothing but go to the lady's room and hope for the best.

Lew had been facing the restaurant entrance, as he always did. The two men, continuing to ignore the receptionist, made eye contact with Lew and slowly began walking toward him.

Lew unobtrusively pulled his pistol out of its holster and rested it in his right hand beneath the table.

Smiling, he said, "That's close enough. You here to spoil my dinner?"

"He has a low and suspicious mind, doesn't he, Iggy?"

"I would say so. Would you care to come with us so we can have a little business talk?"

"I'm busy tonight. Try me another time."

He could see the two of them slowly inching inside their jackets for their pistols.

Smiling again, Lew said, "Make one false move, and you're both dead."

"Did he just threaten us?"

"I believe he did."

With that, the two of them quickly pulled out the pistols. They were quick but not as quick as Lew, who pulled his trigger twice—one for each in their chests.

Pandemonium reigned! Pam, on hearing the shots, rushed back to see Lew calmly seated where he had been. The two men who came his way were on the floor and not moving. Their guns ended up like in a movie, each equidistant from their immobile hands.

The restaurant had emptied of patrons entirely. The waiter tentatively approached Lew's table.

"We'll skip desert tonight," Lew said.

"There will be no charge tonight, sir."

"I'll have to wait here till the police come."

"I don't anticipate much of a crowd the rest of the evening. You know these two gentlemen?"

"No, and I don't think I'll have that opportunity again."

Pam had reseated herself with a pulse rate of 120.

"Care for anything else to eat?" Lew asked her.

"Don't think so. Kind of lost my appetite."

"Waiter, could you bring us a couple glasses of Chardonnay while we wait?"

"Right away, sir."

Chapter Sixty-Eight

May hadn't seen her friend for almost a month even though they worked in the same hospital. A vision she had about the lady prompted the desire to see her.

During lunch break May went to Janice Barkely's floor. Each was glad to see the other.

"It's been so long!" May said.

"It has, and you're going to get married! How exciting. I've had a few changes myself."

"That little nurse on Three-West got friendly?"

"Do you know Dr. Greene?"

"Cardiologist, isn't he? Never met him. I've heard nothing but good things about him."

"His wife died about six months ago—leukemia."

"He's in his forties, isn't he?"

"Two years older than I am. I've always liked him, and we were discussing a patient when he abruptly asked me out to dinner. I accepted. He looked so . . . so sad."

"Didn't that spoil your credentials?"

Janice laughed. "There's more. I had a grand time. I presumed he was just looking for a sympathetic heart. I was wrong. We talked about everything but his late wife. I brought her up myself. When he talked about her, I could barely hold back my tears. He took me back to my apartment, and I hugged him. I've been out with him several times since. He was first in his med school class. He's smart as a whip but humble. Not a trace of arrogance. Kind, thoughtful, considerate."

"You do know he's a male, don't you?"

"Do I ever!"

"You don't mean?"

"It turns out I'm a switch-hitter."

"So any thoughts about marriage?"

"Yes, and about having a child. His wife was infertile."

Once lunch was over, May said, "Did I mention I had a vision about you last night?"

"No. Am I going to like this?"

"I saw you in bed with a newborn—"

"A newborn?"

"You interrupted me—a newborn on both of your sides."

"Twins?"

"I believe that's what they call them."

"Do you mind if I tell him about this?"

"Not at all. That might be the stimulus that makes it all happen."

Chapter Sixty-Nine

Pam and Luigi sat at their table in the restaurant. Pam let out something that was a cross between a laugh and a snort.

"What was that about?"

"It's ridiculous. We're casually sipping Chardonnay with two dead men at our feet."

"You're right."

The restaurant had closed its doors. They knew the police would if they didn't.

"There they are."

Three cops and a captain entered. They went straight to Luigi's table.

"Good evening, Captain Hook."

"Luigi, Luigi, do you look for trouble, or does it look for you?"

"A little of both, probably. This is my good friend, Pam Spicer."

They were all pleased to meet her.

"I gather these two men were uninvited guests?"

"Oh yes. They came in through the front door, ignored the receptionist, and scanned the room. They saw me, referred to a picture in their hand, and made straight for our table. I'd never seen either of them before. I unholstered my fully licensed pistol and kept it under the table. We chatted a bit, and when they started to draw those guns you see on the floor, I shot them. I had the foresight to ask Ms. Spicer to go to the restroom before all this transpired."

Forensics had arrived by then and had cordoned off the area.

"They're both dead," a new member of the team said.

Luigi handed his gun to the captain, who checked the cylinder.

"Didn't waste any bullets here, did you?"

"They're expensive—waste not, want not."

With the iPhone-standard equipment, the two deceased men were identified on the spot.

"Both had long criminal records, top heavy with violence."

"May we go?" Luigi asked.

"Of course. I'm going to recommend you for a service award for ridding the neighborhood of these two."

"Any cash in that?"

"No. Just an 'Attaboy.'"

On their way home, Pam asked, "Weren't you antagonizing that captain, calling him Hook?"

"No. That is his name. I think he likes it."

Luigi chose not to wake his father. The discussion could wait till then, when reprisals could be formulated.

Pam was surprised she slept so well that night. Luigi? Not so well.

CHAPTER-SEVENTY

Breakfast at the Silencio home

"We had an incident at the restaurant last night."

"An incident?"

"For want of a better name. Two heavies came in with the intent of killing me."

"They were unsuccessful, I see."

"I'd never seen them before, and they needed a picture of me to recognize me. I spotted them the moment they came through the door. I sent Pam to the lady's room and had my gun in hand under the table. As they were pulling out their weapons, I shot them both. Our old friend, Captain Hook, showed up. With their phone cameras, they identified them right away. Long criminal records, heavy on violence."

"Not tied to the Capellas?"

"Not that we know, but who else could it be?"

"Pam, if you're through eating, would you please go see if we made the morning news?"

She didn't want to hear what they had to say anyway and promptly left the table.

"Father, we cannot let this go unpunished!"

"How can we know who to punish?"

"Who else besides the Capellas?"

"We've had peace for over five years. We should be slow to blindly retaliate."

The housekeeper interrupted them. "Sir, a mister Capella on the phone for you." He put the call on speakerphone.

"Tony, quite a surprise to hear from you under the circumstances."

"I heard the news of the shooting last evening. They were not our boys—absolutely. They were freelance guys, so we inquired around about them. They were not there to kill Luigi. They were there to kill Luigi's current girlfriend."

"That's crazy!" Luigi said.

"Not when it's your previous girlfriend, Lilly, who hired them."

"Damn!"

"We have done our part, as have you, to keep the peace the last five years. With seven million people around, there's plenty to go around. We are in the position to see that there is no recurrence."

There was a pause. "That would be a favor not to be forgotten," Mr. Silencio said.

"We would call it a goodwill gesture."

"Weren't we smart to get these phone scramblers installed?"

"Indeed."

Lilly disappeared the next evening and was never seen again.

CHAPTER SEVENTY-ONE

It was past time to interview Sterling Post's cousin and the boy's mother.

Bobby Rizzo made an appointment to meet with them at their house. He introduced himself and was offered a seat.

"Had you heard that your cousin Sterling was shot last night?"

"My sister called me late last night. I haven't heard from her today yet."

"I have to ask—Turk, where were you at eight last evening?"

"At a movie."

"Which one?"

"Regal on Philips Highway."

"What movie is playing there now?"

"The new *Mission Impossible* was the one I saw."

Bobby had seen it already. "Did you reserve a seat there?"

"I did, but I didn't have to. Only thirty or so people were there."

"Do you have your ticket stub?"

"I think so. Want me to get it?"

"If you would, please."

"Mrs. Thomas, you were home alone last evening?"

"As usual."

"Did anyone call you on your phone between eight and eleven?"

"No."

"What time did Turk come home?"

"I don't know. He's always quiet. I took a sedative last night."

"Why?"

"I was worried about Sterling."

"Here it is." Turk handed Bobby the ticket stub.

"What part of the movie did you like the best?"

"That part where the helicopters were about to fall off the cliff."

What that meant was that he had really seen the movie.

"What time did you get home last night?"

"Maybe eleven or so."

"What kind of a car do you drive?"

"Ten-year-old Ford. Looks like an antique."

"How's your health, Mrs. Thomas?"

"Lots better than my poor sister. I'm fine."

"She's in heart failure?"

"That's what they say."

"When did you see her last?"

"Week ago, I guess."

"What do you make of both of her sons being shot so close together?"

"Well, they're both gay. Some people around don't like that much. Me, I couldn't care less."

"I don't care either," Turk interjected.

"Do either of you own a gun?"

Both shook their heads negatively.

"Do you have a job, Mrs. Thomas?"

"I'm a hotel clerk at a Hampton Inn."

"How about you, Turk?"

"I'm a full-time student at the junior college."

"To sum it up, you were home between six and ten."

"Yes," she replied.

"And you left home about seven and returned sometime after eleven?"

"Yes, sir."

"Thanks for your cooperation."

On the way home, too late to go to the Police Memorial Building, Bobby thought, *I need to find out if anyone saw or didn't see the old car.*

CHAPTER SEVENTY-TWO

Sterling's parents had been up all night at the Gainesville hospital where their son was clinging to life. He had sustained a chest wound that required a segmental resection after three pints of blood. He was sent appropriately to the ICU after his recovery room stop off.

Chest incisions are painful postoperatively. Sterling's injury precluded a thoroscopic approach. He was heavily sedated but rousable. His chances were now better than ever because his medical team had done everything right. He had youth on his side too.

One of the boys who had gone with Sterling to the Gainesville Social Club was sitting with Sterling's parents.

"He's gonna make it. He's tough."

"We all hope and pray so."

"I guess it's not my place to tell you, and maybe it is. Sterling isn't gay. Far from it."

"He told us—"

"For him it's been a social tool—girls swarming all over him trying to change his persuasion."

"Are you sure?"

"Very."

They didn't ask for further clarification.

"Well, if he survives, maybe we'll get to be grandparents after all."

CHAPTER SEVENTY-THREE

Luigi pondered long on what to tell Pam about the origin of the shooting. He had made his own vow never to lie to her. Withhold some things, yes. Decline to answer, yes. He didn't know how much violence she could tolerate. The restaurant shooting was isolated and did not portend any repeat. He would see how she responded to that. He found himself in the unfamiliar position of dwelling on what would be best for her, not himself.

Breakfast, after the Capelli call

"Did you have enough excitement last evening?" Luigi asked.

"Oh, yes, the Chardonnay was splendid."

"Would you like to hear what it was all about?"

"Pass the eggs, and lay it on me."

"You heard of a former girlfriend of mine named Lilly?"

"Yes. Your store manager likes me a lot better than she did her."

"She took a dim view of my ending the relationship. She hired those two goons to do the shooting."

Pam continued to eat her eggs. "Does she get her money back?"

"Likely not. She's changed her location. Turns out they were hired to shoot you, with me as an afterthought."

Pam was still eating her eggs. "I take it she didn't leave a forwarding address?"

"No, but we had nothing to do with that. Our competitors, the Capellis, found out about it before we did. They didn't want any misunderstanding about the origin. We do not plan to do anything about it."

Pam finished her eggs. "But as a goodwill gesture, the Capellis will, right?"

Luigi was astonished!

123

"Likely so."

"One of those 'live by the sword, perish by the sword' thingees?"

Luigi nodded his head.

His father, who had remained silent at the table, spoke up, "Does this scare you off?"

"Not even close. Loved the eggs."

CHAPTER SEVENTY-FOUR

Sterling Post had turned the corner during the night. His endotracheal tube had been removed, and he was to be discharged from the ICU. Mike Blake was the Gainesville detective who would interview Sterling, who was full of pain medicine but could still communicate.

"I'm Mike Blake, your local neighborhood cop. You feel like hell?"

"Yes."

"Any idea who made you feel like hell?"

"Sorry, no."

"You were found just outside of your apartment. Do you recall that?"

"I think I had just put my key in the lock when a voice at the back of me called my name."

"Any words besides that?"

"No."

"Anything unusual about the voice?"

"Male, young."

"Did you see him at all?"

"There's a big azalea plant there. He seemed to have come out from behind it—I'm not sure though."

"Have you made anybody mad lately?"

"Not that I know of."

"No shared girlfriends—anything like that?"

"No."

"No arguments lately with anyone in your complex?"

"None at any time. I think he called my name to be sure I was who I was. He was after me, but I have no idea why."

"Your parents are outside. I need to talk with them. I may see you again in a few days."

"I'm sorry to be of so little help."

"I'm thinking we'll find the guy. We'll damn sure try!"

"Mr. and Mr. Post, I'm Lieutenant Mike Blake, Gainesville Police. I just talked with your son. He's doing remarkably well. He offered no help at all as to who the assailant might have been. Can you help me there?"

They looked at each other and shook their heads. "No, unless, well, he let it be known that he was gay when he really wasn't. He said it worked wonders with his social life—something about their trying to change his 'persuasion,' as he put it."

"He didn't mention any disagreements or controversies he'd had?"

"No. They said his wallet was intact, so it wasn't a random mugging."

"No, sir, it wasn't. He looks great now, considering how close to death he was yesterday."

"You don't suppose whoever did this will try again, do you?"

"No, but we're putting an officer in place in case I'm wrong."

CHAPTER SEVENTY-FIVE

Bobby and Buddy were in their office discussing their winners and losers. The current loser that bugged them the most was the late Victor Post and now (almost) his brother, Sterling.

"I heard this morning that the Post boy is going to survive. Mike Blake is on the case."

"He's a first-round draft choice. We've worked with him before. Any progress on the case?"

"Not yet, but he's remarkably upbeat about it. The shooter was a young (whatever that is) male. He called out to Sterling as if to be sure who he was. One shot to the chest. Mike will be interviewing the nearby residents today. A lot of them are students with variable schedules."

"If he had died, his parents would have had Turk's mother as the next of kin. If Turk were the shooter, he would have needed a round trip time of what? Four hours? That's supposing he knew right where to go and when Sterling would be alone. He did have the movie ticket stub, which meant he wouldn't have had time to make the round trip."

"Do you keep ticket stubs?"

"No. It could have been a ploy wherein he saw the movie in his off time and tore the ticket up himself. That would have given him plenty of time for a round trip."

"We're going to canvas Turk's neighborhood about him and his car. No way to check on the theater parking lot. I'm sure Mike will be doing the same over there. We sent him a picture of the car this morning."

"How'd you get that?"

"Got it back when the brother was shot. We had only his mother's word he was home when the brother was shot. None of the neighbors could refute it. Do you remember that Alec Guinness movie way back where this peripheral nobleman determined he only had eight or so relatives standing between him and the dukedom—or whatever you call it—and he set about killing them all off? *Kind Hearts and Coronets*. That's the name of it."

"I'll be sure to look it up."

"Did we ever get a look at the will of the Post boys' parents?"

"I don't think so. I guess we should. I expect they're in Gainesville now."

Chapter Seventy-Six

The second day after Sterling was shot, he was doing so well that he was discharged from the ICU and transferred to a regular floor. The chest tube he had been given was removed uneventfully. His pain was decreased, but his pain meds were still required.

"You need to go back to your own activities. I'm on autopilot now—crisis over," he told his parents.

They were receptive to that after his doctor told them he was out of danger. They had slept very little the past two days.

"Do we need to take him to our home when he's discharged?"

"That might be good for a week or two. His outlook is good whatever you do."

"Can he ride in a car, or do we need an ambulance?"

"Being a short trip, a car should do fine."

Sterling resisted going to his parents' home, but not very much. The prospect of being overwhelmed with care and love was more than acceptable to him.

The following day Bobby Rizzo called the Post home.

"Mrs. Post, I hear Sterling is doing very well."

"Our prayers were answered. Have you made any progress about his assailant?"

"We've ruled out a number of people, but no, we do not have a prime suspect yet. Do you have a copy of your will at your home?"

"Yes. Do you need to see it?"

"We haven't come close to a motive yet. We thought your will might give us a lead."

"You can see us anytime."

"How about now?"

"Let me check with Hal."

Mrs. Post called out, "The police want to see our will. Okay with you?"

"Of course. It's pretty simple."

"Is it still simple if Sterling hadn't survived?"

"Oh my God! It couldn't be—?"

"I'll be there in twenty minutes. Thanks for your cooperation," Bobby Rizzo said.

"That 'per stirpes' has some meaning now that Sterling has clarified his, what do they call it? Persuasion?"

Hal broke the silence. "Your sister and her son would have been next, even without a will."

"I've been thinking the unthinkable too."

CHAPTER SEVENTY-SEVEN

Bobby read the will. It was simple as advertised. It hadn't been amended since Victor Post had died, but it allowed for that anyway.

"My two sons (names noted), equal parts. Per stirpes had been included."

There was no mention of a beneficiary beyond the two boys and their offspring, if any.

Hal's will left a trust that inured to his wife, as long as she lived, then passed on to the two sons.

"You have no other living relatives, do you, sir?"

"No. None."

"And you have only one sister who, in turn, has one son?"

"Correct. Her parents are deceased, and I have no knowledge of my own."

"What kind of a relationship have you had with your sister?"

"We were never what you could call close, but I've had no problems with her."

"None?"

"Well, I sensed an undercurrent of envy when her husband died and had such a small estate while we were being frugal and making plans for our retirement. Nothing concrete there, and nothing really of late."

"How about her son?"

"He was unkind to small animals when he was little. My sister was indifferent when I broached her on it. I don't know of any real problems with him otherwise."

"Statistically, that's not a good credential."

"So I've read."

"We'll keep in touch with you. Be sure to let your sister know Sterling will be at home for a few days."

"The doctor said a couple of weeks."

"I know. Tell her a few days, anyway. Don't tell a soul that you will have a policeman in your house for a few days."

"You mean?"

"Just a trial balloon."

CHAPTER SEVENTY-EIGHT

In his youth, Damon Franks had aspired to becoming an FBI agent. He was agile enough and smart enough to do so, with a little help from his friends.

He went directly into entering a criminal-degree program as soon as college was feasible. What with some help from his parents and student loans here and there, he cobbled together a workable program.

His enthusiasm never failed him, and he obtained his degree with high marks. He had an uncle who had been in the FBI for over twenty years. Whenever he would be with the uncle, Damon would pump him for stories of his experiences, and his uncle was very forthcoming and encouraged him to stay the course.

The FBI liked applicants who had previous experience in law enforcement, so Damon applied for the Jacksonville Police Program, was accepted, and completed it with honors.

He didn't have any breathtaking experiences in the next two years, but he did receive high evaluations from any and all.

He did not resign from the police force until he had been accepted into the FBI program. Here again, he excelled.

There was a shadowy federal unit that didn't seem to report to anyone, and he caught their eye. It was called the Paramilitary Research Unit. Its function was to explore and investigate avenues that were outside the usual counterintelligence areas. He wasn't entirely sure what his job would be, but it didn't take long for his first assignment to surface.

"Mr. Franks, are you happy with your job so far?" his supervisor asked.

"Yes, sir, even though I'm not quite sure what it is."

"We research areas that are not overtly military issues but which could be of benefit in any foreign enterprise involving the USA."

"Such as?"

"Such as your first assignment."

Damon was excited!

"You came from Jacksonville, Florida, didn't you?"

"Yes, sir."

"We have heard reports of a nurse down there who has prescient abilities. Do you know what that means?"

"Predicting the future, I believe."

"That's correct. It is probably fictional, but if by chance, she does have this trait, we would wish to employ her to evaluate any and all enemies of the state."

"That would be worthwhile, if true."

"We want you to go meet her and make an assessment of her abilities. You have two weeks or longer, if needed, to complete your task. Your cover is that you're on a covert mission for the FBI."

"But I'm not. Correct?"

"Not exactly."

"When do I leave?"

"Tomorrow morning. Your flight leaves at ten-thirty. You'll be staying at the Hampton Inn off Baymeadows Road."

"I'm familiar with it."

"If you think you will be needing a weapon, I'll be giving you the location that could accommodate you."

"Weapon? Is there something you're not telling me?"

"No, no. Just a precaution. I don't think you'll need one."

"I report to you?"

"Yes. Be vague about our organization. We don't like the limelight."

"Understood."

"I know your uncle. He's a big fan of yours."

"And I of him."

"Any questions?"

"Do you have any data on the nurse?"

"Oh yes. Here's her story."

Damon's supervisor handed him an envelope.

"Does this incinerate a minute after I read it?"

"Not this time. Good luck. Be sure to take your *Salacia* device with you."

"We're good buddies."

"You like the holograms?"

"Very realistic."

"I've found myself talking to her like she's a real person."

"I wonder if she has a boyfriend."

"Ask her sometime."

CHAPTER SEVENTY-NINE

Damon's Hampton room was ready for him when he checked in at noon. It was entirely adequate and clean. He decided to call Ms. Stover and try to arrange a meeting with her, perhaps that evening.

He had to use his title to get through to May's floor.

"I need to speak to Ms. Stover, please."

"Whom may I say is calling?"

"Damon Franks of the FBI."

May hadn't quite gone to lunch then and came to the phone.

"Ms. Stover, I'm Agent Franks, and I'm with the FBI. I would like to talk with you at your convenience about your prescience. Our office is aware of the two potential major catastrophes at your hospital that were prevented by your timely actions."

"They've been somewhat exaggerated."

"Our office wants me to see if you would be attracted to doubling your salary and moving to Washington."

"No, sir, I would not. I am currently the happiest I've ever been in my life right here, and I'm getting married in a couple of months. I'm sorry you came so far to find that out."

"I have really enjoyed my three hours here. Could you do me the big favor of having dinner with me this evening? I go back to Washington tomorrow."

"I've already made plans to dine with my fiancé."

"Could Matt and you join me at a place of your choosing?"

She liked the FBI agent and figured it would not please his superiors if he went back empty-handed.

"You know his name, I see. Unless he has an objection, we'll meet with you. You don't do kidnapping and all that stuff, do you?"

"Not often. It would mean a lot to me."

He gave her his cell phone number and closed the circuit.

"What's up with this FBI stuff, May?" her fellow nurse asked.
"If I told you, I'd have to kill you."
"That would spoil my day."

CHAPTER EIGHTY

It was fine with Matt. He was curious about the visit. May planned on being mostly cautious. Damon was looking forward to another encounter with this beautiful gifted lady.

Matt was gracious and felt not the least bit threatened when they met at LongHorns. Other than for some mild envy of Matt, Damon was cool.

After they were seated and had, all three, ordered salmon, May told both of them that many of her visions never came to pass and others did. She had no way of differentiating the two outcomes. The two hospital deficiencies her vision had illuminated were fortunate, to say the least, but other visions that followed did not come to pass. It was an incomplete "gift," at best.

"Would you have any interest in moving to the Washington area?" Damon asked Matt.

"I'm a successful Southern boy. I love it here, as does May."

"I never was much of a salesman," Damon stated.

"Neither am I, so I became a nurse—the patients come to me unsolicited."

"Sooner or later, people need new cars," Matt offered.

"I envy your happiness and situation. Are there any more at home like you?"

"No, and Mom's glad of it."

"The salmon was excellent. We do have great restaurants in DC. I'll free up you lovebirds now. I do appreciate your having dinner with me. If your percent of accurate predictions improves, here's my card. The offer would still be open."

May gave him a gentle hug as they parted and wished him well. Matt shook his hand, and did likewise—the wish, not the hug.

"Well, what do you think of him?" Matt asked May on the way home.

"He's lonesome, but he will establish a relationship with a girl he sits next to on the plane tomorrow."

"You putting me on?"

"No."

"I know I've seen you before," the girl next to Damon on the plane said.

"I would never have forgotten you if we'd met before."

"Oh lordy! And you don't wear a wedding ring."

"Neither do you."

"I did once when I was seventeen."

"I'm sorry. I have a bad habit of steering conversations into troubled waters."

"That's almost poetic. What do you do when you're not talking to strange women?"

"I'm in the FBI."

"Do you know Reggie Stage?"

"Sure. Older FBI gentleman. I like him a lot. How did you come to know him?"

"Dad's easy to get to know."

"He's not . . . ?"

"Yes, he is."

CHAPTER EIGHTY-ONE

"Well, what's your assessment?"

"She indicated that many of her visions do not really come to pass, and she can't tell the valid ones from the other ones at the time."

"No percentages offered?"

"No, sir. I suspect she's more accurate than she lets on. She and her fiancé are altogether happy and in love. They like it where they are, and Washington has no appeal to either of them."

"The double money didn't affect them?"

"None whatsoever. Where's Reggie Stage these days?"

"I believe he's on the president's protection team. Why do you ask?"

"I sat next to his daughter on the way back."

"As I recall, she's a real fox. Attorney, isn't she?"

"Uh, I never got around to asking her."

"Bad form, Damon."

"Hers isn't!"

"Isn't what?"

"Her form, sir."

"You did find out how to contact her, didn't you?"

"I did."

"Strike while the iron is hot, boy!"

"Is that an order, sir?"

"Absolutely!"

CHAPTER EIGHTY-TWO

The next morning

"You were sure in the shower a long time," Matt said to May.

"I know. I was having the most vivid vision of my life."

"About what?"

"There will be an attempted bank robbery this afternoon."

"Do you know where?"

"SunTrust Bank on Baymeadows."

"Well, that sounds specific enough. Who you going to call?"

"The only cop I know is that Buddy Short, but he's a murder detective, I believe."

"Call him anyway. He'll get the right people on it—if he believes you."

"He should, and he will."

"Other than that, Sherlock, how'd you sleep last night?"

"Dreamed of the love of my life, which was silly since he was right there beside me."

"You know, sometimes you bring tears to my eyes."

"Didn't mean to."

"Then you can just kiss them away."

She did that, and then they departed for their respective jobs.

Coffee break.

May got to Buddy easily, which surprised her.

"Of course, I remember you, Ms. Stover. You have some more violence to report?"

"One of my visions, I'm afraid. There will be an attempted robbery this afternoon at the SunTrust Bank on Baymeadows. Two men."

Buddy knew when to be serious. "I guess I don't have anything left to ask. I take you seriously."

"This vision left me no doubt at all."

"I'll see that it's unsuccessful. I presume you still don't want credit?"

"Please! Under the radar!"

"Rick, Buddy here. I just had a tip, which I believe, that there will be an attempted bank robbery this afternoon at the Baymeadows SunTrust building."

"Can you tell me the source?"

"The source wishes to remain anonymous. Go get 'em, Rick!"

"Will do."

CHAPTER EIGHTY-THREE

Bobby Rizzo was able to get a search warrant for Iris and her son, Turk's, home.

The considered opinion at headquarters was that Turk had killed one uncle, gravely wounded another, and was well on his way to an irregular inheritance. Only problem was that there was no proof. Perhaps a bit of searching would be efficacious.

"Good morning, Mrs. Thomas. I'm Sergeant Rizzo, as you may recall. I have a search warrant for your house and grounds. We'll try not to be disruptive."

She snatched the warrant from his hand and scanned it.

"Why? What's this all about?"

"Just routine, ma'am."

"It damned sure isn't routine for me!"

The two officers who came with Bobby carefully searched the interior of the house. An hour later, they had finished and had found nothing of consequence.

"Where is your son now?"

"He's at the grocery store for me."

"Will he be back soon?"

She considered lying about it but decided not to.

"Anytime now."

"We'll wait."

"You've already turned the house upside down, including his room."

"Yes, but not his car."

Anxiety for Mrs. Thomas!

Five minutes later, Turk pulled in. Bobby had stationed one of the officers where he could intercept Turk if he decided the police cars were a threat to him.

"Mr. Thomas, you may go on in the house. I'll be searching your vehicle."

"You can't do that!"

"Yes. I can. Go on in, please."

What little bluster he had managed in the parking area, evaporated when Turk found the other policemen there.

"They had a warrant, Turk," Mrs. Thomas said acidly.

"Neither of you have a gun, as I recall."

Two heads nodded.

"The reason we're here is that Turk's car was identified as being in Gainesville the night his cousin was shot. Had you loaned your car to anyone that night?"

"No! It was in the parking lot at the movie house where I was. You saw the stub."

"You stubbed the ticket yourself and saw the show another time."

Both Turk and his mother were wild-eyed and red-faced.

"Is there anything either of you want to tell us?"

"Certainly not! This is all a misunderstanding!"

The officer who searched Turk's car came in.

"Looky what I found."

CHAPTER EIGHTY-FOUR

Lieutenant Rick Rogers took two other officers with him to the SunTrust Bank on Baymeadows Road. It was noon. The tip had said afternoon, so here they were.

The two officers stayed in their unmarked squad car as Rick, not in uniform, went inside. He asked to see the manager.

"Yes, sir. What can we do for you today?"

Showing the manager his credentials, Rick said, "We had a tip that your bank might be robbed this afternoon. I have two other officers outside."

"Robbery? We've never had a robbery here!"

"Maybe you won't today either, but we'll hang around just in case I'm right."

"Oh please do! What do you want me to do?"

"It's important that all of you do just what you would ordinarily be doing. We don't want to spook the guests."

"Should I tell the others?"

"Absolutely not. It has to seem natural here. Some of your employees probably don't have the fortitude you do."

The manager straightened up. He may have flitted up a bit more than usual, but by and large, he kept the faith.

2:00 PM

The two cops in the unmarked squad car saw them first. Two men alighted from their car. They scanned from side to side, making sure there was nothing to deter them. There was a third man in the car, and he kept the motor running.

One more quick surveillance at the back of them, and then they entered the bank, donning ski masks as they did so.

The men came in shouting, "This is a bank robbery. If everybody does what they're told, nobody gets hurt. These guns are loaded. Now, everyone on the floor, please."

All but one obeyed. A little old lady with a cane didn't seem able to comply.

One of the robbers ran over to the wall and brought a chair for her.

"Thank you, young man."

"Welcome."

"For God's sake, get on with it!" his cohort shouted.

"Now, ma'am, I want you to put all the paper money you can reach into this satchel. If you push that buzzer down there, my associate will start shooting people at random. If you sneak in one of those exploding ink devices, I will wait a month and come back and kill you. Are we clear on this?"

The clerk nodded her head up and down vigorously. Her mouth was so dry she didn't know if she'd ever speak again.

Thirty seconds later, her wildly shaking hand shoved the satchel out her window.

"Now see, folks, we have our money. You've been good, and nobody's been hurt. Just one more thing—wait five minutes before you do get up."

Turning to the older lady on the chair, the man said, "You get up whenever you want to."

"Come on!" his partner yelled.

"Out the door, off with the masks."

"The idiot turned the engine off!"

CHAPTER EIGHTY-FIVE

Pam Spicer had spent the last three months with Luigi in his father's home. She was comfortable with the two of them and what the men did for a living. She even enjoyed working at the import store they owned. It was rapidly becoming fish-or-cut-bait time.

"Lou, what's the end point with the two of us?"

"Will you marry me?"

Talk about your bait cutting!

"Just like that?"

"Just like that. I would have asked you sometime back, but I needed to see that I could make you happy here. I believe I can."

"I want to make you happy too."

"You're still willing to have my children?"

"That's what brought this to a head. I seem to have missed a period."

"You mean you're . . . you're . . . ?"

"Looks that way."

There were tears in Lou's eyes. She'd never seen any before, so she joined him. They embraced for the longest time, though it didn't seem so.

"Will your father approve?"

"He's been goading me on for two months. He says I'm not getting any younger and all his friends already have grandchildren."

They went to the living room where Lou's father sat reading.

"What's the book about, Dad?"

"It's about a poor old man who never had any grandchildren."

"Why do I not believe that?"

"Actually, it's a book of Italian poetry."

"You can hardly speak it anymore."

"Ah, but I can read it. You two look happy."

"We want to get married."

"Now if I were a crusty old man I'd say 'It's about time,' but since I'm not one, it delights me."

"There's a bonus aspect too."

"Such as?"

"Such as if all continues to go well, you'll be getting that grandchild."

His father did his best to hide his own tears.

CHAPTER EIGHTY-SIX

The officer had a pistol dangling from a pencil.

"That looks very much like a pistol, George."

"That's what I thought."

"Didn't you both say you didn't own a gun?"

Turk exploded. "We don't. If you found that in my car, someone planted it there!"

"Where was the pistol, George?"

"In the locked spare tire well."

"I didn't know tire wells were locked."

"This one was."

"Anything either of you want to tell us now?"

"We want a lawyer," She said.

"That's probably a good choice. I'm afraid both of you need to come with us."

"She doesn't have to. She doesn't know anything about it. It was all my idea. I wanted to support her with an inheritance. Who saw my car in Gainesville?"

"Most everybody. There may not be another eleven-year-old car in the city."

"I'll go down with you, if I may?" the crestfallen mother said quietly.

"How did George know to unlock the tire well?"

"A car that old wouldn't have anything of value to put there or anywhere else."

"Clever officer," Buddy stated.

"Of course. I trained him," Bobby declared with fake modesty.

Buddy called all the interested parties, telling them that the case had been solved, with the perpetrator being in jail. If asked, he told them who the perp was.

"You got everybody informed?" Bobby asked him later.

"Yes. Had to leave a message a couple of places."

"How many thank-yous?"

"I lost count after none."

CHAPTER EIGHTY-SEVEN

The officers suggested that the driver of the getaway car turn his engine off. Seeing the size of the pistols pointed at him, he complied. Seeing that he was unarmed, they told him to stay put and confiscated the car keys in case he wished otherwise.

The two robbers were all set to raise hell with their little old driver, who was neither jolly nor quick, when two men with pistols confronted them. Having put their own guns away, all they could do was raise their hands and curse eloquently.

Rick rushed out of the bank with his pistol drawn, which he promptly holstered when he saw the situation to be well in hand.

What with three men in custody, Rick called for the paddy wagon, which arrived ten minutes later, and off they went.

Before that, the bank manager had surfaced and was giving out thank-yous to any and all. Every customer that exited the bank then had their cell phones on full throttle. Well, there was one exception. The little old lady who had sat in the chair walked carefully up to Rick.

"Most fun I've had in a month of Sundays!" she told him and toddled off.

May was about done with her shift when she received a call from Buddy.

"The three would-be bank robbers are in custody, and no one was injured. The community owes you a debt of gratitude, as do I."

"Good citizenship. You will keep all this to yourself, won't you?"

"Yes, I will. Send me a wedding invitation."

"You're already on the list."

CHARACTERS

Barney, Don—Nemesis of May
Barkely, Janice—Nurse friend of May Stover
Blake, Mike—Nemesis of May
Franks, Damon—IRS agent
Heller, Matt—May's fiancé
Post, Vic—Another nemesis of May
Post, Sterling—Vic's brother
Rizzo, Bobby—Police sergeant
Sales, Sam—Yet another nemesis of May
Short, Buddy—Police lieutenant
Silencio, Guido—Bouncer
Silencio, Luigi—New York (shady)
Stover, May—The main character
Tenor, Wally—Not another nemesis? Yep!
Thomas, Iris—Sister of May's mother
Thomas, Turk—Iris's son

OTHER BEESON BOOKS

Death in the Recovery Room
Kidnapping, Drugs and Murders, Oh My!
Death by Plastic and Revenge, Oh Dear!
Death in the Preserve
Death and the Lottery Family
Redemption
The Wages of Sin Is —
Damaged Merchandise
Max and Friends
God's Little Deputies
Reaffirmation
Recycled
Asbestos